Mask-Querade

Edited by

H.K. Hillman

and

Roo B. Doo

The Twelfth Underdog Anthology from Leg Iron Books

Halloween 2020

Contents

Foreword   H. K. Hillman   7

Occupational Hazards   Emma Townsend   9
The Games We Play   Emma Townsend   17

The Do-Gooder   Daniel Royer   25
Bad Wishing Well   Daniel Royer   31

Milltree Guest House   Marsha Webb   59

Fly Babies   Gayle Fidler   63

Small World   H.K. Hillman   71
Bagboy   H.K. Hillman   79

Dust Mote Halloween   Wandra Nomad   85

What Time Do You Finish?   Roo B. Doo   93

Horseman of the Year Award   Mark Ellott   103
Anonymous   Mark Ellott   111
The Wisdom of Cnut   Mark Ellott   121

Afterword   Roo B. Doo   131

About the Authors   133

Foreword

H. K. Hillman

Halloween again. My favourite anthology of the three published by Leg Iron Books every year. In past years my inspirations for stories have been local. 'Treeskull Stories' came about because I found a deer skull embedded in a holly tree in the garden. 'The Gallows Stone' referred to the discovery of an actual gallows stone used in the construction of an extension to this house in 1835. 'Well Haunted' came about after being informed that the house's water supply comes from an ancient holy well.

This year, the inspiration is global. The entire planet has gone mad. Over something that is not nearly as bad as it appears, and which has spawned a test that is remarkable only for its unreliability and control measures so draconian and so utterly useless that one has to wonder what is really going on.

It may well be that all of this will come to light before Halloween, or it may not. In the meantime, every cloud has a silver lining and this insane and unprecedented situation has inspired a few of the stories in this book.

It has also inspired the title, Mask-querade. A mask behind a mask. How many will you have to remove before you find the true face? Is there even a face under there? Unfortunately, the only 'mask' story I've written is already in the very first Underdog Anthology. It would have been a good fit for this year.

Well, we have some excellent stories for this Halloween and as has become something of a tradition, we have another new author to introduce. Emma Townsend opens this collection with two tales, followed by some of the regular contributors you'll be familiar with if you've been following this series.

Dive in, take a look around, and see if you can find your way back out.

Occupational Hazards

Emma Townsend

Day three. She woke in Aunt Celia's bed, naturally and quietly, the gentle patter of light autumnal rain against the window bringing her to full consciousness. It was comfortable and serene under the sage and lavender covers, a little oasis of warmth and calm, and as she pondered the day ahead, she found her thoughts wandering to problems past and possible problems future. *But no, that's no good*, she thought, and rose briskly and business-like to begin the day.

She was wise to the cat now, and descended the stairs watchfully. Sure enough, there were stringy brown entrails on the fourth step, a green organ she didn't wish to investigate on the third and a thin line of semi liquid excrement on the first. She tiptoed over and around these with a good grip on the bannister and called out as she reached the ground floor. "Hector? Hector!"

The round head of an old tom cat appeared slowly around the door jamb, his body following sinuously behind his lopsided sneer. She guessed she had disturbed him mid-groom and stifled a laugh at the lip caught on his front tooth. He rubbed his entire body along the glossed wood and came slowly toward her, his green eyes showing but a slit of pupil as he squinted up at her expectantly. He blinked.

"Hector," she said in the most serious voice she could muster, "this is not acceptable."

The cat turned and began a long, low stretch with his back legs stiff and his tail erect, displaying his puckered pink anus directly toward her before sauntering back to the front parlour.

Her thoughts fled to the animal remains on the carpeted stair and wondered if she should bury or bin them. There really wasn't enough left over today for a proper funeral, which was a shame. The rest of the deceased, she supposed, was in Hector's belly and before she could halt her mind from wandering she imagined she could solve that particular problem by burying the cat himself, and thereby the mouse within him. *No. Oh no.* she thought, and deliberately stopped and closed her eyes to recall Aunt Celia's wise words.

"We don't harbour bad thoughts. We recognise them, we give them a nod, but we do not begin a conversation and we certainly don't invite them in. Bad thoughts cannot be domesticated."

"Bad thoughts cannot be domesticated," she echoed, "bad thoughts cannot be domesticated," and she stepped toward the kitchen for a full bodied coffee then slipped, dramatically, her left foot shooting forward and her right foot high in the air as a slipper came bouncing off her forehead. She heard her hip slap onto the tiles and in the second before the pain hit, she looked down between her knees and noticed a smudged puddle before picking up the scent of rank urine. *Bad thoughts cannot be domesticated,* she thought, *and neither can that damn cat.*

It was rather cool in the kitchen without her slippers. She took off her dressing gown, which had become a little soiled at the hem, and inspected her pyjamas as well as she could. They seemed to have escaped the mess. She struggled with the washing machine door, trying to get the dirty items in, but the handle wouldn't budge. She switched the machine on and off again, and once more at the plug but had no better luck, so dumped the gown and slippers in a bundle on the floor with a sigh. *Later.*

The tap rattled and gurgled before producing a slim stream of water and she pumped the soap dispenser twice. A streak of blue shot from the nozzle, but not into her hand. She looked about for the soap, puzzled, then tried again without success before unscrewing the bottle head and tipping a little straight onto her palm. When she came to dry her hands on a towel, she found the dripping dollops of blue soap waiting for her. Picking it up gingerly with a thumb and forefinger, she dropped the towel onto the dressing gown pile then promptly dried her hands on her pyjama top.

She got an electric shock from the kettle. Not huge, just enough to snatch her hand away and shake it like the devil. She examined her fingers closely. There was no damage, but they were definitely dry. She reached out again, hesitantly. Click. She waited awhile for the kettle to begin its crackling roar, one hand cradled against her breastbone, the other rubbing her throbbing backside as she began to ponder her suitability for this housesitting job. She collected herself abruptly and admonished her drifting mind for chasing negative thoughts. Surely she could handle a little housekeeping, being a grown woman after all, and a voter now that she'd turned eighteen.

"A vote," she said, "I have a vote." Her voice seemed small and lost. A mouse in the belly of a house. She cleared her throat, "I said, I have a *vote.*"

A sheet of rain dashed against the window and bare twigs from an overgrown bush in the back yard rattled on the pane, tapping and scraping, overpowering the noise of the kettle. It looked like the weather was worsening, and she thought there may be a stormy night ahead. Good; it would keep her company in the dark quiet of the house tonight. It was Halloween, and to deter the trick or treaters, she would leave all the curtains open with not a bit of light or noise to attract them. She found nothing more relaxing than listening to bad weather beating its way about the rooftops and chimneys, and the idea cheered her somewhat when she considered how a cold rain might put a few of those little beggars off.

She took a mug from the draining board and placed it carefully beside the kettle. She reached toward the fridge, but stopped mid-air as she recalled the interior light, which had decided to turn strobe, and the general pervasive funk of the whole thing. Coffee would be served black today. She slowly unscrewed the top of the instant coffee and scooped an oversized portion.

There was a regular tapping at the window, and she looked up to enjoy the cloudy wet view once more. Her eyes met another pair staring straight back and she jolted, the spoonful of coffee granules cast across the counter, and the jar itself knocked over to spill a full half of its contents.

"Shoo!" she said, startled and struggling for composure, "Shoo! Go home!"

The crow leaned low and pecked once more at the windowsill before turning to flap awkwardly across the garden.

She looked at the horrid mess, which she knew would be a horrid sticky mess in no time. The granules had scattered across the entire kitchen worktop, spreading over, between and atop all her aunt's various jars of homemade jams, chutneys, pickles and preserves. None were labelled, and some made her feel nauseous to look at. The cleaning would be an unpleasant job. It could wait.

At last, with a hot drink, she eased herself down at the kitchen table. She took care to lower herself gently onto the chair, partly due to her sore bottom and partly due to not wanting to fall off it again, and ran her fingers through her hair. The bump from her encounter with a swinging cupboard door on her first day was still tender. She blew on her coffee and took a tentative sip. There was a little knot of worry beginning to work its way around her insides, so she made an effort to relax her shoulders, take a deep breath, and focus on her favourite daydream.

Her university, wherever it was, she was sure would be a good old fashioned red brick, with acres of green lawns, winding paths and stairwells. She would have a room there, with art posters on the walls and a tiny, cramped desk for study. There would be people, so many people doing so many things. Clubs, sports, debates, nightlife. She would sit at the back of her lectures, taking copious notes, finding the uncommon angle and outshining her new friends with uncommon grace... but her memories intruded, showing Aunt Celia at this very table leaning close enough for her to see the burnt and brittle ends of her wispy hair, a physical reminder of her aunt getting just a little too close when blowing out candles.

"What do you want to go there for?" she had said, *"All those strangers. As for Psychology, it's not even a proper subject. I'll give you psychology: it is the nature of a human to be human and a cat, by nature, is a cat. They act as they always have and always will. There. I just saved you three years. Mark my words, they'll squeeze everything useful out of your head, then fill it up with graphs and charts and statistics. You'll come out twice as daft as you went in."*

She looked deep into her drink, blowing the steam gently, feeling her guts begin to tense and churn again. She raised the mug to her lips and felt a sudden loss of weight as the body of the mug fell into her lap, dumping its scalding contents all over her groin and legs as her fingers continued to curl about the useless handle. She leapt up with a sudden intake of breath and the chair legs squealed across the tiles. She cast the handle onto the table top as the mug fell to the floor and began to pick at her pyjama bottoms, pulling the hot fabric away from her skin.

"Bastard, bastard, bastard," she hissed. Her eyes began to sting and prickle with the promise of tears.

She leaned across the table, snatched her phone and keys from an otherwise empty fruit bowl and made for the front door, careful to avoid Hector's mess this time, and slammed it behind her with more force than strictly necessary.

Barefoot, she took the garden path on the balls of her feet, hopscotch style. The iron gate had worked its way loose in the wind, so she secured it properly with the latch behind her, pulling it level with the spiked railings. She began a slow march along the pavement, counting the houses as she walked past. The rain was icy and refreshing, the gusts of wind lifting her hair and dropping it to leave it plastered against her cheeks. She felt calmer and looser already. When she had counted to six she stopped and glanced about. There was not a soul to be seen, so she leaned against a post box and scrolled through her contacts for Aunt Celia's number.

"Sweetie! A Happy Halloween and Shocking Samhain to you! You'll never guess where I am. All the girls are here. Girls, it's our kid on the phone…"

She heard a number of coos, wails and jolly 'hellos!' faintly at her end. "Auntie, I'm sorry, I didn't want to disturb…"

"I'm glad you called, actually. I've been thinking about that gate. It keeps working its way loose, so if you could see you way clear to tying it up with a bit of string or something? I don't want a repeat of last year. Remember the lad who tripped over the crazy paving? Fell on the rails?"

"Yes, I remember. Straight through his…"

"Terrible mess, wasn't it? Anyway, how are you? How are things? How's Hector?"

"Hector's fine, he's just Hector. It's everything else, though. I mean..."

"Just a minute, I'm moving away for a bit of privacy. There we are. Fire away."

"Oh Auntie, I'm so sorry. I don't think I can manage. I mean, it's the chair, it's the soap, it's the bloody washing machine, and the crow…"

"I know that crow, he's a bugger."

"And I nearly cried today. I'm not sure I can do this."

"Alright, settle yourself now, settle. I'm going to give you an easy fix. Let me start with something you already know. When I am gone, the house will be yours."

"What?"

"Well, it has to go to somebody. Who else do I have? Here is another thing you already know: university is not for you. Not now. Maybe in a couple of years when you've grown into your skin a little. Look at yourself, sweetie, crying over a crow. How are you going to manage miles and miles away?"

She tipped her head to the grey sky, feeling the sting of tears once more.

"And here is a thing you don't know, are you listening closely?"

"I am," she said.

"Then here it is: come and work for me, finish your training, and you can own the house now. It's just a change in timescale, is all. We'll do the paperwork next week. How's that for a solution? A household needs a head; it's not a bloody democracy. Stop taking all this silly nonsense and own it. Just own it. Sweetie, I'm sorry, I have to go now. Breakfast is on the table and the coven's waving at me. I'll call you tomorrow!"

With that, the line went dead and the screen blanked out but the world about her was full of motion, sound and life.

A cyclist passed her by on the pavement, riding with both hands tucked deep into his jacket pockets. He looked her up and down, leering.

"Shit the bed, did we?" he grinned.

She looked down at the coffee stain on her pyjamas then watched his retreating back for a heartbeat or two, gauging the wind coming from the west *just so*, and a ripple of a pothole *just there* and focussed. Sideways he crashed into the dripping privet hedge, losing his bike. There was a small folly of a brick wall under there somewhere.

Be free, bad thoughts, fly free, she purred in her head to cover the sound of his complaints because if you can't bend the rules on today of all days, then when could you? She smiled, because that is in the nature of witches, especially the younger ones, and looked long and hard at the house as she walked up. She rested a finger on the gate.

String she thought at it, and felt the smallest of shivers. Not enough. *How about a nice long length of plastic coated washing line, wound round and round and round*, she thought, and the gate gave a noticeable shudder.

"Right then," she said.

In an old and cold stone building, long past use, Celia gathered her skirts to step over the pew and seat herself at the altar.

"Well?" said Esme.

"Did you do it?" asked Sybil, breathlessly.

"Are you free of the cursed place now?" said Minnie, reaching for the brown sauce.

"Ladies, ladies," said Celia, "far be it from me to be counting chickens before they are hatched but," she delved a fork deep into an eyeball and held it aloft, "I give you success!"

Some slapped their thighs, and some slapped the table, but there was a raucous noise all about for it is in the nature of elder witches to cackle.

The Games We Play

Emma Townsend

ACT 1

Kenny laid Frankenstein's monster gently on the table and said, "Howzat?"

The other three looked on, unimpressed.

"I don't get it. What is it supposed to be?" asked Mai.

Kenny sighed and tipped his head to the ceiling with his eyes closed. "It's a piñata," he said slowly, emphasising every syllable, "I told you I was bringing one."

"Then how come it's not a donkey?" said Sebastian, "Or maybe a llama? Aren't they supposed to be llamas?" he glanced over at Tom for confirmation, but Tom Wolfe took a large sip of his green smoothie and settled back in his chair to signal he was out of the conversation, the furniture creaking under his massive frame.

"I still don't get it," said Mai.

Kenny turned his round and ruddy face towards the girl, "It's made of paper and hollow inside. You bop it with a stick until it breaks, then everybody has to scrabble around on the floor for the goodies stashed inside. Got it? I can't articulate it better for you."

"Alright," she said "Chill out. What else you got?"

"Glad you asked," said Kenny and hefted a large and obviously light bag onto his lap. He held the ends open and invited Mai to put her hand in, "Want to go fish?" he said.

"Hell, no," she replied, and flashed the small solitaire ring on her left hand.

"Well, well, look who got engaged; and there's me thinking you'd die an old maid." Kenny shrugged and pulled a long, looped piece of twine from the bag, "A noose for Frankie here," he said, laying it next to the piñata, "Took me a whole day to make it, and best of all – these bad boys!" He produced a cellophane packet of wrinkly red chili peppers and shook them jauntily. "Listen up carefully folk, for these are no ordinary chili peppers, these are Komodo Dragon peppers straight from my hometown of Newmarket."

"A snack on the train up here?" asked Sebastian, raising his dark eyebrows.

"Even better," smiled Kenny. "It's a Halloween Trick or Treat. I wiped one around some of the glasses and mugs... and things. A Halloween Russian Roulette, maybe?"

"Oh, you bastard," said Mai.

"Easy now, my little Mai Ling. Lingy Lingy Lingus," said Kenny and flicked his tongue at her suggestively.

"I am *so* going to kill you," she hissed, and made to rise from her seat.

"Time out!" called Tom Wolfe, loud and clear as he leaned forward to put his elbows on the table which tilted alarmingly, making the others lean back.

"Time out, guys," he said quietly as he placed his empty glass down and began to gesticulate with loosely cupped hands the size of breakfast bowls. "Remember why we're here. It's Kenny's first day back as an innocent man. No charges, remember? Now, I'm sorry there's just the four of us for the welcome and housewarming, but lockdown is lockdown and it can't be helped. Let's be grateful we're in our last year here, and we can bubble together, ok? What could connect four old friends up better than a party, huh?" He looked each of the others directly in the eye, with only Mai holding his stare. "So," said Tom, "This is how it's going to play – we're going to grab a couple of beers..."

"I'll wash the cans first," said Mai.

"For sure," he replied, "we could do without the capsicum fear factor..."

"And wipe out all the glasses," she said, eyeing Kenny.

"Absolutely, but my main point is," and he held up one sausage-like finger to discourage further heckling, "We're going to get this show on the road. Mai does some washing up, Sebastian gets the music set up, and Kenny does his hangman thing with Frankenstein."

"Where do I hang him from?" asked Kenny.

"Try tying him from the light fitting, somewhere near the top – trumps drilling a hole in the ceiling," said Sebastian.

"Spot on, Seb," said Tom Wolfe, "Bingo! So now we put these plans into operation. Time to fall-out and get moving. See you back here in an hour when it's properly dark; I'm heading up for a wash. Alright? Go!"

ACT 2

It was long past sunset by the time all four met back in the common room of the Victorian terrace. Curtains had been drawn that did little to stop any draughts, and low wattage bulbs highlighted the patchily painted plaster on the unevenly built walls.

Sebastian was last in, wearing a fresh shirt and a wide grin. He pushed dark curls off his forehead as he handed a flat bungee rope with hooks to Tom Wolfe. "Is this the sort of thing you were after?"

Tom pulled the wide elastic as if to test its strength and said, "Just the job." He pulled a chair from the table and set it in the middle of the room underneath the dim bulb and swinging piñata. "Alright, party boy, let's have you." and tapped the back rungs of the chair invitingly.

"What, me?" said Kenny.

"You're the party boy, aren't you? The prodigal son?" said Tom, "Shut up and set your arse on the chair. It's time to play some party games."

Kenny hesitated, he looked about to see Mai relaxed with a Taboo and lemonade, her backside propped against the table top. Sebastian was grinning widely at him, his hands tucked into the front pockets of his jeans. Tom gestured to the chair again.

"Fine," sighed Kenny, and sat down.

In a conversational tone Mai said, "I heard the first years have put signs on the windows – 'Let Us Out' and 'HMP UNI'. Can the university really do that, Tom? Keep them locked up?"

Tom was attempting to tie the bungee rope around Kenny without restricting his breathing too much, "Not legally," he said, "Anyone can go skipping out any time and visit the pub. All they've done is introduce a kind of fine for breach of contract. You could argue it the other way in court of course, if you're willing to pay and take the risk. God, Kenny, you've put on some weight, breathe in a bit." He managed to tag the two hooks together finally and said, "Bullseye, that's done, mate," tapping him gently on the shoulder.

"You see," said Tom, stretching back up to his full height, "Criminal matters are different. To get your time in court, you don't pay: it's up to the police having to prove a solid case to the Crown. It's all down to evidence. They won't bring it forward if they don't think they can win. Ain't that so, Kenny?"

19

"What game are we playing here?" asked Kenny, his suspicions aroused, "Just give us a clue, will you?"

"The game? That's the sixty-four thousand dollar question," said Sebastian, his perfect teeth looking supernaturally white against his black stubble, "Here's your clue – do you know how many times you've pissed off everyone in this room?"

"Think of it as a kind of Truth or Dare," said Mai, still leaning easily against the table, "Only It's more of a Truth and Reconciliation, really."

Kenny made to move out of the chair, but Tom's weighty and intimidating hands held his shoulders down, making him slump in defeat. "Time to get our game on!" said Tom.

ACT 3

Sebastian pulled a piece of paper from his back pocket and began to read the charges laid down upon it;

The incident where Tom's rugby kit was hidden in the freezer, his football boots smeared inside with sardines, the clingfilm over the toilet bowl, duct tape on the bathroom tap, every other stitch in the crotch of Sebastian's best trousers cut, plastic flies in the fridge, hidden phones, pink dye in the washing machine, itching powder in Mai's underwear drawer...

"I've kept a mousetrap in there ever since," said Mai.

"I know," replied Kenny.

A unified and wordless sound of disgust came from the other three.

"You creepy bastard," said Tom, leaning down close to Kenny's ear and putting greater pressure on his shoulders. He glanced up at Sebastian, "Time to move on."

Sebastian gave Tom a single affirmative nod and walked quickly but silently in his baseball boots to the window, reaching behind the curtain for a wicked looking knife. He paced back to face Kenny with confidence in his lithe frame.

"Since it's pointless going any further with that, we're going to get to the crux of the matter," said Sebastian, running his finger along the flat width of the blade. His voice dropped low, "Tell me what happened that night with my sister."

Kenny began to struggle in earnest, squirming until his chair reached a tipping point, but Tom held him all the while, gently guiding him back into position with an easy strength, careful not to bruise or pinch him in any way. "Steady now, little buckaroo," whispered Tom, "We don't want you hurting yourself."

"I'm not doing this anymore," said Kenny, his voice high and panicked, "I'm not doing these fucking charades."

"I appreciate your frustration," said Sebastian as be began to pace gracefully back and fore, the knife tapping against his thigh, "but you must appreciate mine. It's been a long eight months."

Although the sweat was beginning to prickle along his back, Kenny sat straighter in his chair, the realisation he was helpless galled him. He was going to fight his corner just as he had the past few months. He was ready. He put on a resigned poker face and said, "I'm innocent, and you bloody know it. No charges. Even the Dean let me back on campus. Shit, I lost months of my life to this and I'm not losing any more. I could have been locked up. It put my degree in jeopardy. Cut me, it doesn't change anything."

"Legally, you're innocent. Legally, I understand that. Tom's explained it to me well enough," said Sebastian, hunkering down low in front of Kenny with one knee on the floor, his knife looking more threatening for being held so loosely, "But you can knock it off with the halo shit because nobody buys it, and you never lost any real time here because of the lockdown and summer recess. Save your tears, fat boy."

"Just tell us what happened between you and my fiancée," said Mai, walking unsteadily over to flash her ring once more, "She's got a ring now that matches mine. The game of life moves on, so," she gave a small stumble and spilt a little of her drink, "You're right – it doesn't change anything, nothing ever can."

Kenny swallowed audibly, "What... a brother, a lover, and who are you, Tom? A long lost Auntie?"

"What am I? No, mate," replied Tom in a level voice behind him, "I just live here."

Sebastian held the knife and began to run the very tip of the blade oh-so lightly along the inner seam of Kenny's ill-fitting skinny jeans. "Tell us what happened with Zelda," he said in breezy tone, as if talking to a child, "Tell us the truth, play your cards right and this will all be over with very, very soon. It's up to you."

"Alright, alright, I get it!" Kenny took a deep breath, as far as the bungee rope would allow, and began.

"It was like this; I woke up sometime in the small hours really thirsty. I came down for glass of coke or something and the light was already on in the kitchen. Griselda was there. She was making a coffee or something. We spoke a little bit and she was smiling and joking. She wasn't wearing much. Just a long tee shirt. I went to kiss her and she didn't move, so I thought…"

Sebastian flashed his eyebrows at Kenny, "You thought what?"

"I thought it was ok. I mean, she turned around and she had nothing on underneath, and so I just…she never said anything or pushed me away. I asked her to come up to my room afterwards, but she just shook her head and I guessed she was maybe a little embarrassed or something, so I went back to bed on my own. Next thing I know, a week later, a fucking *week* later, I get a visit from the police."

"Yeah," said Mai, "Somebody called the coppers on you. Guess who? You see, right after you went to bed, Zelda put on her coat and boots and ran straight back to the Halls of Residence to scrub herself clean in the shower. She ran. All the way. I never knew anything until the following Sunday."

Sebastian ducked his head down to make eye contact with Kenny, "You fucked her over the kitchen sink. *Or something.* Did I get that right?"

"Yes. I'm sorry. I'm sorry. I'm so sorry!" Kenny's voice was beginning to break.

"I call time," said Tom Wolfe and unclipped the bungee hooks with a sharp snap.

ACT 4

Tom ruffled the hair on the top of Kenny's head. It was damp with perspiration. "Sorry to put you through that, Kenny," he said, "but we had to know. It had to come from the horse's mouth. You're a good sport, you know that? Bloody balls of steel, too." He gave him a rousing slap on the back, "Come on, let's get you a drink."

Kenny pointed a finger at Sebastian, "What about him and his knife? You think I'm just going to forget that?"

"It's a prop," said Sebastian, and plunged the knife into his palm where it wrinkled and bent, "Don't tell me you got fooled by a bit of foam, you daft git!"

Kenny pulled the tail of his shirt to his face, wiping away the sweat from his forehead. "Oh, Man," he said, "I nearly shit myself!"

Sebastian opened his arms wide, "You forget I played Iago in Othello last year. I'm just an actor waiting for his big break."

"Move over, Kenneth Branagh! Come on," Mai called to Kenny, and gestured to the table filled with cans and bottles, "The drinks are on me tonight. Damn, but your face was a picture!"

Kenny smiled for the first time, and began to relax. He mixed a rum and coke and held the glass high, "Cheers! Happy Halloween! You got me good and proper."

"High time we got this party started," said Tom, "Put on some Halloween blockbusters, Seb. I'm going to find something to bust that piñata with."

Bobby Picket's 'Monster Mash' was playing when Tom came back with a cricket bat.

"You're not going to use that, are you?" said Kenny.

"Damn straight," said Tom, "Watch me."

"Hang on – wait, wait, wait. I've got to record this. Somebody lend me a phone," said Sebastian. "Mine's busy playing the music." He took Mai's device from the table without permission or complaint, and began to circle the room with it, taking in the general scene.

Mai was leaning in a wobbly fashion with her hand against the door frame, her thumb dangling over the light switch. She raised her glass for the camera before it swooped to film the alcohol table. The lens then focused on Tom and Kenny in the middle of the room. Kenny red-faced and dancing a half-hearted twist to the music with his glass still in hand, and Tom looking manically pleased with a cricket bat over his shoulder.

Sebastian moved to the corner of the room and said, "Whenever you're ready."

"I'm going to give a countdown," said Tom Wolfe, "Are we all still good to go?"

"Aye," said Kenny.

Mai slowly blinked once in acquiescence.

"Ready here," said Sebastian.

"Right, then," said Tom Wolfe, glancing at Kenny with his fat, sweaty face shining in the light, "In three….two…."

Out went the light and round came the bat for a little Murder in the Dark.

What's the time, Mr Wolf?

It's playtime:

Donkey, Bop It™, Scrabble™, Articulate™, Go Fish, Solitaire, Twine™, Old Maid, Newmarket, Russian Roulette, Connect Four™, Fear Factor (TV), Wipeout (TV), Hangman, Top Trumps™, Bingo, Operation™, Fallout™, Go!, Draughts, Taboo™, Skipping, Risk™, Tag, Bullseye (TV), Give Us A Clue (TV), The $64,000 Question (TV), Cluedo™, Truth or Dare, Game On! (TV), Rugby, Football, Sardines, Mousetrap™, Baseball, Pointless (TV), Tipping Point (TV), Charades, Frustration™, Poker, Halo™, Jeopardy (TV), Game of Life™, What Am I?, Zelda™, Play Your Cards Right (TV), Guess Who?™, Sorry!™, Snap, Balls of Steel (TV), Pie Face™, Othello™, Big Break (TV), Blockbusters (TV), Monster Mash™, Cricket, Countdown (TV), Murder in the Dark

The Do-Gooder

Daniel Royer

He inserted the razor blade into the bite-sized candy bar. With a warm knife, he carefully spread chocolate over the insert markings. He held the candy bar under a lamp, examining it through his bifocals. The candy bar looked pristine. He placed it back in the wrapper, adding a little adhesive to seal it. He tossed it in the bowl with the others.

It was Halloween, and Mr. Morgan had spent most of the day making additions to the trick-or-treat candy. On his desk sat a box of razor blades, a bag of heroin, a jar of rat poison, and a tube of glue. It was slow meticulous work, and it aggravated Mr. Morgan's arthritic hands, as well as strained his eyes. It was worth it. He carefully opened a tube of Pixie Stix. He sprinkled heroin into the tube, lightly shaking it. This too he sealed with glue.

Mr. Morgan was a widower, and he had lived in that home on Maple Street for almost fifty years. Every year he and Martha had decorated the house real spooky on Halloween. They would carve pumpkins and, of course, pass out candy to the trick-or-treaters. Every year they would go to the store and buy an assortment of candy, and put it in a bowl shaped like a black cat. They would let the trick-or-treaters choose their desired candy out of the bowl. The same black cat bowl now sat on Mr. Morgan's desk, holding his surprise candy.

This would be Mr. Morgan's first Halloween without Martha. He decided to keep their Halloween traditions. He decorated his house extra spooky and carved even more pumpkins. The pumpkins sat on his front porch. Mr. Morgan even bought the same candy from the same store. Except this time, the candy had a few surprises. He grabbed a small bag of Skittles, eyeing the rat poison.

Mr. Morgan knew that parents often inspected candy before allowing their children to consume it, some even throwing out candy that didn't appear to be properly sealed. Mr. Morgan squeezed out some glue on the Skittles wrapper, closing it up with the rat poison. His surprise candy sure wasn't going to have *that* problem.

It seemed that at the end of every Halloween season, there was always a newspaper story of some kid getting poisoned by surprise trick-or-treat candy. The frustrating thing, according to the writers of

25

these articles, was that it was usually difficult to track down the culprits. The average trick-or-treater often knocks on hundreds of doors on Halloween night, receiving several pounds of candy. And because the average trick-or-treater is so hopped up on sugar and hijinks, he often doesn't remember which doors he knocked on, or even which blocks he walked. Police detectives were usually stumped. Mr. Morgan was counting on this. He was also counting on his reputation in the community, for Mr. Morgan was known as something of a do-gooder.

For the past year, Mr. Morgan had been extra nice to the neighborhood children. He patted them on their heads as they walked on the sidewalk in front of his house. He exchanged pleasantries with their parents and gave them flattering compliments about their front lawns. He attended the children's baseball games and made appearances at all neighborhood barbecues. He laughed with the children during times of joy, and cried with them during times of sadness. Mr. Morgan even made substantial donations to the children's hospital and orphanage. It was certain that the next morning, November First, when the surprise candy had taken its effect, everyone in the community would know that Mr. Morgan was not the one who committed this evil deed. Mr. Morgan was a do-gooder. He would be above suspicion.

And in case he wasn't, well, that's what the hand gun on his nightstand was for.

Officer Katie Hummingbird did not look like a cop when she wasn't wearing her uniform, nor did she much look like a cop when she *was* wearing it. Officer Katie was twenty-four years old, and stood at five foot one inches tall. She was a pretty girl with red hair which she tied back smartly in a ponytail, and when she smiled, which was often, her dimples were as deep as oceans. She spoke with a high Dora the Explorer squeak. Even her name *Katie Hummingbird* did not sound much like a police officer's name. It was true that Officer Katie Hummingbird did not seem like a threat to those that did not know her. But to those that knew her best, which were big bad criminals, Officer Katie Hummingbird could not be more terrifying.

Less than two years out of the police academy, Officer Katie's arrest record doubled any other policeman's in the city. She already had four notches on her gun belt, which also doubled the notches of the other cops. Though her arms were rail-thin, Officer Katie could out-bench-press all the men in the police station. On her first week on the force, Officer Hummingbird dropped a scumbag who had pulled a nail gun on her. The other cops joked that she was tough as nails. Her reputation grew over time as she bare-knuckled it with barroom brawlers nearly twice her size, and dueled with gang members who had more tattoos than Katie had inches in height. Officer Katie was the arresting officer of their local serial killer Grisham Howdy who had terrorized the city for over a decade—that reign of terror ended when Officer Katie entered the force. Grisham Howdy was scheduled to get gassed by the end of the year. Officer Katie had also cracked the case of the mayor's kidnapped son. Recently, she had single-handedly taken down the city's most vicious drug cartel, from which her gun muzzle was still warm.

There were rumors that Officer Katie Hummingbird would be police chief by age thirty. Katie ignored these rumors and did her thing—which was put on a police uniform, hop in her sled, and blow street-scum away. What mattered to her was that she was doing good for her community. The mayor had given Officer Katie many commendations during her short tenure on the force. He had also given her many assignments. Today, Halloween, he had given her a fun assignment as a sort of "Thank You." Her assignment was to award a certificate of appreciation to a local do-gooder.

The do-gooder was a recent widower who was reported to have patted children's heads, attended junior baseball games, and cried with kids during times of sadness. The do-gooder had also made large donations to the children's hospital and orphanage. The city was appreciative of the do-gooder. In a very different way, the do-gooder's contributions to the community rivaled even that of Officer Katie Hummingbird. Officer Katie was not threatened by this. She was happy for the do-gooder. As far as she was concerned, community service was a wonderful thing, whether it was patting children on the head, or filling bank robbers with bullet holes. It was all good with Officer Katie.

Officer Katie Hummingbird was pleased with her assignment. Her orders were to drive over to the do-gooder's home, and hand him his special certificate. Maybe she would even take a selfie with him. Perhaps, if the do-gooder was a Halloween celebrant, she would get a piece of candy out of him. She had a soft spot for chocolate bars. And when her assignment was concluded, she would hop in her sled and drive the streets, making sure that the trick-or-treaters were safe. And if Officer Katie Hummingbird saw any evil-doers threatening that safety, well, there was room on her gun belt for another notch.

She studied the mayor's printed instructions. The do-gooder's name was one Cyril Morgan. He lived on Maple Street. Officer Katie hopped into her sled and drove over.

Mr. Morgan sealed off the last chocolate bar. He tossed it in the black cat bowl with the others. The bowl was now full. The box of razor blades was empty—so was the bag of heroin and jar of rat poison. Mr. Morgan looked out the window. The sky was pink—dusk approached. The trick-or-treaters would be out soon. Mr. Morgan rubbed his eyes. It had been a long day. He was tired, but giddy. The fun would soon begin.

Suddenly the doorbell rang. Odd. It was a little early for trick-or-treaters. They usually came out after dark. Mr. Morgan looked through the peephole. At his doorstep was indeed a trick-or-treater. It appeared to be a girl dressed as a police officer. Mr. Morgan smiled. He actually had butterflies in his stomach. It looked like the fun would start now.

Mr. Morgan picked up the bowl of candy and headed for the door. He stopped just short of it. He put the bowl down and grabbed his handgun, tucking it in his waistband behind his back. *You just never know. There could be some crazy parents around who weren't too appreciative of his special candy offering.* Mr. Morgan picked up the bowl and opened the door.

The trick-or-treater was older, maybe even a teenager. She had red hair pulled back and dimples. She was cute, pretty even. Over the years, Mr. Morgan had seen many trick-or-treaters, including trick-or-treaters dressed as police officers. He had to admit, even though this trick-or-treater was a teenager, he had seen five-year-olds that looked more authentic than this one. Mr. Morgan doubted she could lift so much as a nightstick. The idea of this "police officer" stopping evil doers was almost laughable. It was actually kind of adorable. He had to resist the urge to pinch her cheek.

"Good evening, Mr. Morgan," said the trick-or-treater in a squeaky voice. "I'm Officer Hummingbird, and I'm here to—"

Officer HUMMINGBIRD! How adorable! Without thinking, Mr. Morgan extended the candy bowl out to her. He was so excited, he just couldn't resist.

"Oh, thank you," said the trick-or-treater. She grabbed a chocolate bar from the bowl—chocolate with a dash of razor blade. "Well, I have the honor of awarding you with a certificate of appreciation for your community service. It's directly from the mayor."

She handed Mr. Morgan a piece of paper. It was indeed a certificate of appreciation. *Wait. Was this girl actually a cop?* His jaw dropped. She continued speaking. Mr. Morgan was not hearing the words.

"...Mr. Morgan? You looked distressed. Is everything okay?"

Mr. Morgan was having trouble breathing. "I... I... I thought you were a trick-or-treater... I didn't know..."

She laughed. Her dimples stood out as she did this. She had a beautiful laugh. She *was* beautiful. "Oh that's quite all right Mr. Morgan. I get that a lot. I'm still pretty young. Again, my name is Officer Katie Hummingbird. I've been on the force for about two years now."

Mr. Morgan was frantic. He could not let her eat that candy. "I'll need to take that candy back, Officer. It's for trick-or-treaters only. I'm sure you understand."

Officer Katie looked hurt. "It looks like you have a pretty big bowl there Mr. Morgan. A piece of candy could sure brighten up my day..."

"I'll give you different candy. I have better candy," blurted Mr. Morgan.

"Don't be silly," said Officer Katie, smiling. "This candy is my favorite." And with that, she peeled the wrapper, and placed the bite-sized chocolate in her mouth. She chewed, then frowned suddenly. A trickle of blood oozed from the side of her mouth. Mr. Morgan and Officer Katie Hummingbird locked eyes. She reached for her gun as Mr. Morgan reached for his.

And the next day, November First, Officer Katie Hummingbird stepped into the police station with three stitches in her lip and a fifth notch on her gun belt. She may have been tough as nails, but she wasn't razor-proof.

Bad Wishing Well

Daniel Royer

Roanoke Island, 1589

They wandered the woods in search of a lost wishing well. The women and children waited back at the fort. A small sentry unit stayed behind to guard against another Indian attack. The others joined their leader for a midnight errand. Their leader was Ananias Dare, and he and the men had trudged through the woods all night. They were getting close now. Dare and his party clambered uphill in the darkness, following the banks of a trickling stream. The stars reflected in the moving water. The men pushed upstream to the water's source. The source of the water would be their destination. Moon beams sliced through the foliage like Indian arrows.

It was All Hallow's Eve, and the shadows of the trees flickered across the faces of the men. They had been on this island in the New World for two years now. The Roanoke Colony was the first English settlement in the New World. Queen Elizabeth had long wanted Britain's presence established in the Americas. The Spanish had already set up shop in regions to the south. Sir Walter Raleigh commissioned the Roanoke project. He put Governor John White in charge. The colony had started out with over a hundred men and women, but was now down to a fraction of that. One by one, like leaves on an October tree they began to die. There was drought. There were food shortages. There were Indian attacks. And then there were the diseases—they tore through the colony even faster than the tomahawks. Morale was low. Suicide was rampant. Governor White went back to England for reinforcements and supplies. He left his son-in-law Ananias Dare in charge. Dare's wife, Governor White's daughter, had just bore their first child—a son. Dare feared for the infant's safety. Roanoke was cut off from its motherland. Ananias Dare and the colony were on their own.

That's when the rumors began—rumors of an ancient Indian well. It started to the south of them in Spanish Florida. Reportedly, the Spanish were searching for a spring that gave eternal life. The Natives down there had spoken of it. The stories trickled north to Roanoke. The Indians of their region kept silent about the enchanted waters. But the whisperings continued among the colonials. There was a wishing well. The Indians only discussed it among themselves. It was their secret. There was even some sort of Indian nursery rhyme that revealed the mystical structure's location. The colonials didn't know the rhyme's translation, only that somewhere out in those dark mysterious woods an old forgotten well offered eternal prosperity to those that wished upon it. The colonials would find it.

Ananias Dare and his men had explored the surrounding woods for nearly a year—and found nothing. Their only discovery was a stream that appeared to have no source. It simply started at the top of a hill and trickled downward. No one could explain the water's origin. The men scoured the woods in search of a source. They came across an old woman who lived in a cave deep in the forest. She sat before a bubbling cauldron. The old woman did not belong to their colony, nor was she Indian. They told the old woman what they sought. What they sought, she explained to them, was the stuff of magic.

"There is an old Indian ode which my cauldron has translated," she said.

"'For wishes to fulfill, just follow river's course,
Atop a lonely hill, awaits the water's source.
A single night a year, the wishing well is seen,
The fountain will appear the night of Halloween...'"

"We were on the right track, gentlemen," said Dare. "What we seek is on the hill above the stream. We shall return to it on All Hallow's Eve." They left the old woman's cave. They would resume their exploration for the well on the thirty-first night of October.

They now continued upstream. The water was just a trickle. The moon towered above the hill's crest. The wishing well would be at the top. The source of the water would finally be explained. They were close. Dare parted the branches of a poplar tree. Silhouetted against a canvas of stars was something that had not been there on their last visit. It was a well.

Ananias Dare drew nearer. He studied the structure. It was made of rocks and stood up to his chest. Water seeped from the ground near the well's base, dribbling down the hill. The magic well was indeed the source of the water. Ananias Dare had found it. He approached it.

"Halt!" someone shouted behind him. Dare turned. A stranger stepped from out of the foliage. The stranger was very tall. Dare could not see him clearly through the darkness. The stranger stepped into the moonlight. It was an Indian. A crow sat atop his shoulder. The bird's eyes glowed orange in the night. Dare flinched.

The Indian stood before him. "What are your intentions with well?" asked the Indian.

"We wish to draw from it," said Dare. "We wish to be fulfilled by its magic."

The Indian shook his head. "No good," he said. "No magic. You leave."

Dare pointed at the structure. "That's a wishing well."

The Indian turned to the well. "That *bad* wishing well." The crow on his shoulder squawked. "Silence, Croatoan!" said the Indian to the bird.

This is a trick, thought Dare. *Of course the Natives would deny us its powers. They want us dead.*

Ananias Dare thought of his infant son. He drew his blade. "We will partake in the wishing well."

The crow squawked and hopped off the Indian's shoulder. It flew to the poplar tree, watching the party from above. The Indian stood erect, eyeing the saber pointed at him. At last he nodded. "As you like," he said. The Indian turned and stepped back into the foliage from where he came.

The colonials approached the stone artifact. Dare peered over its rim. Several meters down, the water awaited, inky and still, its surface reflecting neither the moon nor stars. Dare could sense the well's magic. He reached into his satchel and drew a shilling. Queen Elizabeth's face was imprinted on it. He raised the coin, holding it over the ancient structure.

"We, the people of Roanoke, wish for eternal prosperity for our colony." The crow squawked once more. Dare turned to the bird. It stared back with orange eyes. A wind blew out. The forest stirred. The surrounding foliage shook. An owl hooted. A wolf howled in the distance. Dare heard the sound of creaking rope. He looked once more at the black water of the wishing well.

And he dropped the coin.

It splashed softly, disappearing below the surface. The crow flew off the tree, screeching into the darkness. The wind stopped and the night turned still once more.

"We will return to the fort now," Dare said to his men. They turned back the way they came.

Two years of death, disease and misery would now be over. The Roanoke Colony would soon enjoy an enduring reign of bounty and good fortune. Dare's father-in-law Governor White would return from England to find the colony thriving. Dare's infant son would live.

Ananias Dare and the colonials headed downhill towards the fort. They followed the stream. The crow followed them in the sky. Acres of wilderness separated them from their destination.

For wishes to fulfill, just follow river's course,
Atop a lonely hill, awaits the water's source.
A single night a year, the wishing well is seen,
The fountain will appear the night of Halloween.

These were the first two verses of the Indian ode, as told by the witch, for a witch is exactly what she was. It was unfortunate that she had kept the third and final verse secret from them.

Their nightmare was about to begin.

Roanoke Island, Present Day

"… And when Governor White returned to Roanoke in 1590," said Ms. Agnes, "he found that the fort was deserted. He searched the woods and all of the surrounding area. The entire island had been abandoned. But what happened to the colony? There were only two clues. Carved into a fence post on the stockade was the word 'CROATOAN.' Additionally, the letters 'CRO' were etched on a nearby tree, as if the writer had been suddenly stopped in the middle of his message. Well, Governor White wasn't sure what to do with that information. What was 'Croatoan,' and what did it mean? All Governor White could do was wait. After all, his daughter, grandson, and son-in-law Ananias Dare were missing. But his family never returned. *Nobody* ever returned. The entire colony had simply vanished. And to this day, no one knows what happened to them… but there are rumors..."

It was Halloween, and Freddy listened to Ms. Agnes with rapt attention as he chewed on a hunk of saltwater taffy. Freddy was a pudgy pale-faced boy of nine years, and he was in third grade at Manteo Elementary. He had lived on Roanoke Island his entire life. The island was off the coast of what was now North Carolina, but in the sixteenth century it was the New World. As everyone knew,

England had tried to set up a colony there. Everybody went missing. The old stockade had been rebuilt since then. It was called Fort Raleigh. Freddy's school took field trips there regularly. Fort Raleigh guarded the entrance to the woods. Freddy had done some exploring in the woods. He once found an Indian arrowhead. Ms. Agnes always said the woods held the secrets to the mysteries of Roanoke. Ms. Agnes was an elderly, but spirited teacher. She had taught third grade at Manteo Elementary for ages. Local legends and folklore were her favorite topics.

Freddy loved all the old spooky stories of his hometown. He loved the history and fables almost as much as he loved Halloween. Halloween was his favorite holiday because he got the most candy. Candy was Freddy's favorite thing. He reached into his backpack and grabbed a bag of rootbeer barrels. He had purchased the candy on his way to school that morning at the candy shop on Dare Street. Freddy stopped at the Dare Street candy shop every day before school. He was able to afford the candy because of the checks Grandma sent every week. Freddy would then take the checks to Mr. LaBarbara at the bank. Mr. LaBarbara would give Freddy cash for the checks. With the cash, Freddy would buy candy. That's how money worked. Freddy shoved two rootbeer barrels in his mouth and continued listening to the class discussion.

"I have many friends and colleagues who are members of the Roanoke Archaeological and Historical Society," said Ms. Agnes. "They have a wide variety of fascinating theories regarding this subject. We get together regularly to discuss this and other topics. But before we get into the evidence found by my colleagues, does anyone have any theories of their own?"

"They escaped the island!" someone shouted.

"If that's true," said Ms. Agnes, "*why* did they escape? And where did they escape *to?* And how did they get there? They wouldn't have been able to make a boat big enough to go very far. Governor White and his party searched the other nearby islands. He also scoured the shores of the mainland. They weren't there. Since then, archaeologists have investigated. My friends at the Roanoke Archaeological and Historical Society tell me that there is simply no evidence to support the escape theory... Any other explanations?"

"They died," someone else suggested.

"Well, that's most likely true," admitted Ms. Agnes. "And it would *certainly* be true eventually. But the question stands: *how* did they die? Disease? Starvation? Indians? And if they all died, where are the bodies? Governor White didn't find any bodies, nor did he find any graves. My archaeologist friends have looked in our woods, and haven't found any graves either... So what else does that leave?"

The class was silent.

For wishes to fulfill, just follow river's course,
Atop a lonely hill, awaits the water's source.

No one dared say it.

"Maybe it's the wishing well," blurted Freddy. The eyes of the room turned towards him.

Ms. Agnes paused, then smiled. "Ah... the magic wishing well..." she said. "The only local folktale more fun than an entire colony disappearing..." The legend of the lost wishing well was a bedtime story every child on Roanoke Island knew, including the nursery rhyme that went with it. The rhyme got passed down with each generation of Roanokers. There were even rumors that the nursery rhyme was *missing* a verse. Maybe even *two* verses. The missing verses had been lost many generations ago—they were the final clue to the well's location, and the reason no one had found it after four hundred years. Ms. Agnes had said that her colleagues were close to deciphering a word or two from the missing verses.

The topic of the wishing well stirred up the class. Ms. Agnes spoke. "Calm down everyone. Freddy was not wrong to bring it up. It's only logical to discuss the wishing well. Here we have one hundred people vanishing under mysterious circumstances, and we also have a centuries old Indian fable of a magic wishing well out in our woods. Could the two legends be connected? My historian friends have looked into it of course. They have different theories on the subject. But let me ask you, class... if this wishing well does indeed exist on our island, how is it that no one has found it, including my friends from the Roanoke Archaeological and Historical Society? And even if it *does* exist, does the wishing well theory make sense? After all, wishing wells are *good*. They make wishes come true. But what happened to the Roanoke Colony was most certainly *bad*. Does anyone have an answer for that?"

Freddy swallowed a handful of horehound candy and tried to think of an answer. The only answer he could think of was that if he ever found that wishing well, he would wish for a lot of candy.

Bud and Truman sat at adjoining slot machines at Mettaquem Casino. Bud played both machines, while Truman watched. The two friends drank. As per his custom, Bud had cashed his paycheck with Mr. LaBarbara at the bank, and then exchanged the bills for quarters at the casino. The sack of quarters rested at his feet as he played. The sack had grown smaller throughout the evening. Mettaquem Casino was operated by a local Indian tribe. It was run by Sitting Crow, the chief of the tribe who each night wore a dark suit, bolo tie, and full on headdress.

Bud and Truman were regulars at the casino. They were in their forties and longtime friends. Bud was an accountant and Truman was a couples therapist. They both made a lot of money. The problem was that Bud liked to gamble. A lot. This meant that he never had enough money to pay for other things like food or mortgages. The Mettaquem Casino was taking all of his money. This irritated Bud's wife greatly. Bud didn't know what to do.

Truman had a problem of his own. He was in love. Her name was Sally, and she served cocktails at the Mettaquem Casino. Tragically, Sally thought Truman was ugly and a dork. She said cruel things to Truman when he attempted to romance her. Truman's love for Sally was unrequited. This caused Truman much pain. Like Bud, he didn't know what to do about his problem.

Bud fed a quarter into the machine. He fed a second quarter into the other slot. Both machines missed. He sighed. "Beatrice is going to get mad if my whole paycheck gets blown on the slots again." He reached into his sack and fed two more quarters. Both missed. He dropped two more. "I'm telling you," he said pulling both levers, "Beatrice and I haven't had dinner all week. Plus I haven't paid my mortgage in six months. Mr. LaBarbara at the bank says he's going to repossess my house if I don't pay up soon. If we lose our house, then Beatrice is going to get real steamed. We've got some pretty serious problems. The odd thing is that it's nobody's fault. Every payday, I watch my money grow wings and fly right into these slot machines..."

He inserted two more quarters and pulled the levers. "I just don't know what to do. I'm doing my best trying to provide for Beatrice by going for the jackpot every night. I even play two machines at a time to double my chances. But Beatrice gets mad anyway. You should hear the names she calls me. She says I'm a loser. I just wish I had more money." He fed a pair of quarters. And then another.

"Don't be too hard on yourself," said Truman, sipping his beer. "Beatrice loves you. And you're lucky to have a fine woman like her. Me? I've got plenty of dough, but I don't have a woman..." He stared at Sally the cocktail waitress as he said this. She was serving the high-roller table. Mr. LaBarbara from the bank sat at the head of it. He was wearing a cowboy hat and had a pile of bills stacked in front of him. It appeared he had just told Sally a joke. She was laughing. Sally never laughed at Truman's jokes. Truman continued: "I've been doing my best to woo Sally. I've told her jokes and I've sung her songs. But she doesn't seem to be interested. Last week I asked her if she wanted to take a walk on the beach with me. She said she wouldn't be caught dead with me on a beach—or anywhere else. I just wish I had the love of a fine woman like Sally." He sipped his beer.

"Well, I'm out," announced Bud. Truman looked over. Bud's quarter sack was empty. "I've got no more money again. I guess I won't be paying this month's mortgage. Beatrice is starting to get hungry. She's going to be sore at me about the money again. I just hope Mr. LaBarbara at the bank doesn't take my home."

Truman nudged him. "Mr. LaBarbara's right over there," he said pointing. Mr. LaBarbara was still at the high-roller table, chatting up Sally the cocktail waitress. She was touching his bicep.

They watched Mr. LaBarbara clear all the money off the table, stuffing it into his pockets. He gave Sally a pat on the rump. She cooed. Mr. LaBarbara smiled and walked over to Bud and Truman. He whistled as he walked. He eyed Bud's empty sack of quarters. "I hope to see you at the bank pretty soon for that mortgage, Bud… Yes sir, the bank has been doing pretty good these days. That's why I can afford the high-roller table. We get lots of customers. We handle a lot of accounts. It's funny to say, but I think my most consistent customer is some kid cashing his grandma's checks. I believe he's spending it on candy. We also get customers who want loans. Some of those customers pay back those loans. And some don't..."

"We know how banking works," said Truman.

"Don't you worry about nothing, Mr. LaBarbara," said Bud, bluffing. "I'll be able to pay you that mortgage money right quick."

"I very much hope so," said Mr. LaBarbara. "You have a beautiful house. It's two stories with a pool, if I recall." He grabbed Bud's beer and finished it. He belched and turned to Truman. "I thought you should know, gentleman to gentleman, that I asked Sally out on a date for Saturday night. Dinner and dancing. Maybe a walk on the beach. She says she's considering it. She says she'll give me an answer tomorrow. I tell you, if I see one of those shooting stars tonight I'm going to make a wish. Remember? Like when we were kids? And brother, if I get my wish, I'll be just about the luckiest guy in the world. I've already got the money. Now, I just need the girl. One's no good without the other. Am I right?" He picked up Truman's beer and finished it as well. He put down the mug and wiped his mouth. He looked at his watch. "Well, I've got to get back home and get the candy out for the trick-or-treaters. Happy Halloween, gentlemen." Mr. LaBarbara walked away.

Bud called out to Sally for another round of beer. She gave Bud and Truman their drinks. Truman paid, tipping her one hundred dollars. He tried to loosen things up with a joke.

"Hey Sally, why did the one-legged waitress work at IHOP? Dammit! I mean, where did the one-legged waitress work?"

"You jerk! My mom has only one leg! And she works at Denny's!"

"How about a date tonight?"

"No way!" she said. "You disgust me, you loser!"

Truman watched her go. "I wish I had love."

"I wish I had money," said Bud.

Truman drank thoughtfully. Something brought him back to his childhood days. He was struck by a notion. "Bud, do you ever think about that magic wishing well?"

"You mean that old legend Ms. Agnes used to talk about in third grade? Sure, sometimes. But even if it exists, only the Indians know where it is."

Truman nodded. This was true. Just then, Sitting Crow, the owner of the casino, walked by them, his headdress feathers fluttering in the air conditioning.

"Hey Sitting Crow," said Bud. "You know anything about that magic wishing well out in the woods?"

"Why are you bothering me with this?" said Sitting Crow. "We're having a record day on the slots." He walked away.

"That Indian knows," said Bud. "He just ain't telling."

"Do you ever think about finding that lost wishing well?" asked Truman. Bud sat silent, pondering this. It was a notion every young boy had once entertained. There hadn't been a summer campfire that didn't include tales of the mythical fountain, as well as dreams of its potential discovery. "It could solve a lot of our problems," continued Truman. "You want money, and I want love. Like Mr. LaBarbara said, one's no good without the other. And if we can't get it on our own, *heck*, we'll just *wish* for that stuff. And the well can't be that hard to find. How's the rhyme go? 'For wishes to fulfill, just follow river's course. Atop a lonely hill, awaits the water's source.'"

"Yeah, but old Ms. Agnes says it's missing some verses," said Bud.

"Well, I say we go out tonight and see about finding it anyway. The rhyme mentions a river and a hilltop. We already have the first two clues. Let's find us that those other ones."

"I don't know," said Bud. "If Ms. Agnes' archaeological pals can't find it, how can we? Plus, tonight's Halloween. Things can get real spooky in those woods."

"Spooky be damned," said Truman. "I'm sick of being lovelorn, and you're sick of being broke. And I don't care if no explorers or archaeologists or ghost hunters can't find that wishing well. You and I are finding it tonight!"

And the boys were just drunk and desperate enough to try it.

It was night and the streets of Roanoke were packed with trick-or-treaters. Freddy stopped under a lamppost to adjust his costume. He was dressed as local legend Ananias Dare, the Roanoke Colony leader who disappeared in the very woods that Freddy could see in the distance. The dark tree-tops were silhouetted by the full moon rising behind them. Freddy thought back to the discussion in Ms. Agnes' class. *What secrets those woods kept?* he wondered. They looked more sinister than usual on this Halloween night.

Freddy shook off these distracting thoughts and focused on his task: the accumulation of candy. Hopefully *a lot* of candy. Freddy stepped onto a porch. A jack-o'-lantern glowed by the doorstep. "Trick-or-treat!" he shouted out. A lady opened the door. She was dressed as a witch. It took Freddy a moment before he realized it was Ms. Agnes.

"Freddy!" exclaimed Ms. Agnes. She eyed his costume. "Isn't that wonderful! You're a little Ananias Dare. How appropriate." Chatter and laughter trickled from inside her home. "Oh, I'm just having a small Halloween *soiree*. Join us. The Roanoke Archaeological and Historical Society are here. We're discussing radiocarbon-dating theories and having cocktails."

Freddy stared at her. "I'm nine years old, Ms. Agnes."

"Oh, how silly of me," she said laughing. "I'm sure a young colonial explorer like yourself would rather be out searching for buried treasures and ancient artifacts."

"No," said Freddy. "Just candy."

"Quite right, my boy. Quite right." She handed Freddy a candy bar. He peeled the wrapper immediately, biting into the chocolate. "So, tell me, Mr. Dare," she said, "have you found that lost wishing well yet?"

"Not yet, Ms. Agnes," responded Freddy impatiently. He had other houses to hit.

"You must tell me when you do." She tussled his hair. "Well, I'll need to rejoin my guests. Our club president was about to tell us about some very unusual findings his team made in Salem, Massachusetts. Turns out those people were witches after all. Happy Halloween, Freddy!" She closed the door. Freddy stood on her porch thinking for the second time that day that if ever found the magic well, he'd wish for unlimited candy.

He finished the chocolate bar and walked off the porch. Freddy had no use for a trick-or-treat bucket. He liked to eat the candy as he moved between houses. Freddy considered himself to be something of a connoisseur in the field of candy, much in the same way that some of the adults he knew were with wine. Freddy enjoyed all varietals of candy. He did not discriminate like some of the kids in his class did. He knew that the boy who sat behind him only ate chocolate, and that the girl who sat in front of him only liked the sour stuff. These ugly candy prejudices offended Freddy to near anger. Chocolate bars, sugary candy, the sour stuff… it was all good with him.

Freddy stepped onto another porch. It was an old Victorian home. A crow sat perched on the porch railing. It stared at Freddy with orange eyes. The black bird made him uncomfortable. He turned away, knocking on the door. "Trick-or-treat!" he shouted.

A man opened the door. He was dressed as Willy Wonka. It was Mr. LaBarbara, the banker that cashed Freddy's weekly checks.

"Well, well," said Mr. LaBarbara. "I see I have a little English colonial on my porch. Wait—is that you, Freddy?"

"Hi Mr. LaBarbara."

"How extraordinary. Now what kind of candy would you like? Caramels, fudge, butterscotch… A jawbreaker perhaps…? I have it all. Just pick your poison. I must tell you, young man, I'm in quite a good mood this evening." He leaned towards Freddy, almost whispering. Freddy could smell liquor on his breath. "Between you and me, Freddy, I might have a date tomorrow night. Do you know Sally? She serves cocktails at the Indian casino."

Freddy stared. "I'm nine years old, Mr. LaBarbara."

"Of course you are. I'm sure at your age you prefer tree-houses, comic books, and soda."

"I actually prefer jawbreakers."

"Excellent choice, young man." He handed Freddy a jawbreaker. Just then, the crow, still perched on the porch railing, squawked. Mr. LaBarbara turned to the crow. "Who's your friend?" he asked Freddy.

"I don't know him," Freddy answered indignantly.

Suddenly the crow flew off the railing and snatched the jawbreaker out of Freddy's hand. It flew off into the night with the ball of candy in its mouth. "My jawbreaker!" shouted Freddy.

"Relax, kid, I'll give you another one," said Mr. LaBarbara.

Freddy ignored him and jumped off the porch. He ran after the bird. When it came to candy, Freddy did not like to leave a man behind. He knew that soldiers also shared this principle on the battlefield. The crow flew up the street. It was heading in the direction of the woods. Freddy was a chubby kid, and not a particularly good runner. In fact, he was the slowest in his class. But on this night he ran like a cheetah. The situation called for it. Freddy zigzagged around the trick-or-treaters. He ignored the aching in his sides.

The crow kept flying. Freddy approached Fort Raleigh, the old colonial stockade that guarded the woods. Etched on a fence post was a secret message left by the Roanoke colonials: "CROATOAN."

Freddy ran past the fence post and the fort. Standing before him were the woods. Freddy had explored the woods aplenty, but never at night. He hesitated, hoping the crow would land. But the bird did not land. It continued over the tree-tops and into the forest.

Freddy followed it.

Bud and Truman stumbled through the woods. They passed a flask of whiskey back and forth. Navigating through the thick tangled foliage of the forest was difficult in the darkness, especially after so much to drink. The boys made do. Earlier, they had discovered a trickling stream. They remembered the old nursery rhyme.

For wishes to fulfill, just follow river's course,
Atop a lonely hill, awaits the water's source.

They decided that the stream they found must be the river in question. They followed the banks of the creek as they staggered up the incline, the slow waters moving past them.

The boys stopped to catch their breath. Truman panted, thinking about Sally and how sweet it would be if he found that wishing well. He scanned the horizon. The stream they were following seemed to be coming from the top of a hill.

He pointed this out to Bud.

"Heck," said Bud. "We was up on that hill back when we were boys. There ain't no wishing well on top."

"We'll just see," said Truman. "The nursery rhyme says it's on top of some hill out here by a river. I'd say this is a pretty good candidate."

A crow flew above them, whipping past the tops of the trees. It had orange eyes. There appeared to be something in the bird's beak. It flew to the top of the hill.

"This is spooky," said Bud. "I think maybe we should leave."

"Just think about all that money you're going to get after we find that wishing well," said Truman. "Besides, there's nothing out here to be scared of." That was when they heard a noise. The boys fell silent, listening closer. It was a thrashing noise. It sounded like someone or something was running through the forest. The thrashing noise was louder now. It was heading right towards them. Bud and Truman trembled. They hugged each other just like they did when they got scared together as children. Suddenly, a boy exploded out of the shrubs in front of them. The boy collided into Bud and Truman, all three parties falling over.

Truman brushed himself off. The boy was fat, about nine years of age, and dressed as a sixteenth century colonial. Chocolate was smeared across his face.

"What are you doing out here, kid?" asked Truman.

"That dang crow," said the boy, pointing up the hill, "took my candy! What are you guys doing here?"

"We're here for the wishing well," said Bud. "I'm going to get rich and my friend Truman is going to be in love. We think that wishing well is right on top of that hill."

"That's where that crow flew with my candy," said the boy. "But I've been on top of that hill before. There's nothing up there."

"Just follow us, kid," said Truman. "Maybe we'll find our well, and you'll find your candy."

Bud offered the kid a sip from the flask.

"I'm nine years old," said Freddy.

The three of them continued uphill, following the stream. They neared the top. Truman parted the branches of a poplar tree. Bathed in moonlight was the wishing well. The crow sat atop the ancient structure, its eyes glowing orange in the darkness. Truman approached the artifact. It was about chest-high and formed with rocks. The crow flew off the well, landing on the poplar tree.

Bud and Freddy joined Truman at the mystical structure. All mouths were agape. Truman leaned over the rim of the well. There was water below. He thought back to Ms. Agnes' tales of Roanoke yore. He said in almost a whisper, "We found it."

"Halt!" shouted someone behind them. The three of them turned. An Indian stood on the edge of the foliage. He was very tall. The crow hopped off the tree, landing on the Indian's shoulder, its orange eyes hissing at them. "What are your intentions with well?" asked the Indian.

Truman cleared his throat. "Well, I want love. My friend Bud here wants money. And this kid, I think wants candy." He looked to Freddy. Freddy nodded.

"No good," said the Indian. "Bad magic. You leave."

"We'd like to make a wish first," said Truman nervously.

"That *bad* wishing well!" The crow, still resting on his shoulder, squawked. "Silence, Croatoan!" he said to the bird. He turned back to the three. "You leave now."

"This is a trick," said Bud. "He wants all the good wishes for himself, just like those Indians at the casino who want all my money."

"Yeah," said the boy. "And I heard those casinos don't even have candy!"

"This is true," said Truman. "And they hire cocktail waitresses for us to get love-sick over."

"What is 'casino,' and what that have to do with well?" asked the Indian.

"It means that we're going to make wishes on that well," said Truman, his confidence back.

The Indian sighed. "As you like." The crow flew off his shoulder, once again landing on the poplar. The Indian slumped back to the shrubbery, disappearing in its darkness.

The three stood before the well. Truman reached into his pocket. He pulled out a Susan B. Anthony dollar coin. Truman was so lovelorn that he thought that Susan B. Anthony looked hot. Bud reached into his pocket to find a coin. He knew that wishes on wells were traditionally made with quarters or dollar coins, but he was so broke that he only had a penny. Freddy reached into his pocket. He found a quarter with taffy smeared on it.

Truman went first. "I wish for love. I wish for the hand of Sally the cocktail waitress. Additionally, I wish to be loved by all women." He dropped the Susan B. Anthony dollar coin.

Bud went second. "I wish for money. Lots of it!" He dropped the penny.

Freddy went last. "I wish for candy. I wish to never be without it." He dropped the taffy-quarter. The crow squawked. A wind kicked up. The woods began to rustle. An owl hooted. A wolf howled. Forest critters stirred. The sound of creaking rope could be heard. The three stood paralyzed. The crow flew off the tree. It screeched into the night. The wind stopped and the forest became quiet.

"Let's get the hell out of here," said Truman. The others agreed.

They climbed down the hill, still following the river. The woods were still and silent. The stroll down the hill was peaceful. The moonlit walk began to calm their fears. They thought about the fulfillment of their wishes. Truman thought only of love, Bud of money, and Freddy of candy. Beyond the stream was the fort and beyond the fort was Roanoke.

Roanoke was where their wishes would come true.

Like the colonials that preceded them by over four hundred years, the trio was not aware of the Indian ode's final verse.

They were about to live it.

The trio parted company at Fort Raleigh. Truman headed straight for the casino. Inside, he saw Sally the cocktail waitress leaning on a slot machine counting her tips. Truman approached her, brimming with confidence.

"How about we go back to my place?"

Sally punched him square in the face.

Bud headed straight for home. He couldn't wait to tell Beatrice the good news. Their money troubles were about to be over. Bud stopped short when he reached his house. A foreclosure sign was on his front lawn.

Freddy headed straight for a residential neighborhood to resume his trick-or-treating. All the houses were dark. He ran to the next neighborhood. Those houses were dark as well. Desperate, Freddy ran to the Dare Street candy shop. It was closed.

Things didn't get much better after that. Once Truman's black-eye healed, he went right back to the casino to ask Sally out on another date. This time she kicked him in the groin. The day after that she maced him. The following day she put a restraining order on him.

Truman was perplexed. Even after his wish, it appeared that Sally was not in love with him. *Maybe he didn't wish right?* The odd thing was, it wasn't just Sally who was not in love with him—it seemed to be *all* women. In fact, virtually every woman he encountered was openly hostile towards him. Truman worked as a couples therapist, and most of his female clients canceled their appointments. Strange women that he passed on the street glared at him—some even *assaulted* him. Even Truman's own *mother* had some cruel words for him when he visited her.

But worst of all was Sally. Truman opened the newspaper one day and saw a wedding announcement. The subjects of the announcement were Sally and Mr. LaBarbara the banker. They would be married the following week.

Bud was having a tough time too. He and Beatrice were now homeless. They were living under a bridge in a cardboard box. Beatrice was furious. Mr. LaBarbara himself had moved into Bud's house. Mr. LaBarbara was now married to Sally. She was living there too, as well as her one-legged mother.

Bud drew a good salary from the accounting firm in which he worked, and decided that instead of spending his money at the casino, he would save his money to buy another house. Unfortunately, his boss forgot to pay him one week. The week after that his paycheck caught on fire when he was careless with his cigarette. The following week a crow snatched the paycheck from out of his hand and flew away with it. So far Bud had been unsuccessful in saving money. Beatrice was getting real steamed.

Bud was confused. Even after his wish for lots of money, it seemed that he had even *less* of it than before. In fact, he had no money at all. *Perhaps he shouldn't have used a penny to make a wish?* What really annoyed him was Mr. LaBarbara. Not only was he living in Bud's house, he was making *additions*. The LaBarbaras had added a third story and a high-dive for the pool.

Freddy was going through a rough-patch as well. The day after the wish, he went over to the Dare Street candy shop. The owner told him he was all sold out of candy. Apparently, this was typical after the Halloween season. He told Freddy to come back next week. Freddy came back the following week and bought a licorice. He stepped outside with the licorice and a crow snatched it out of his hand. Freddy chased the bird, but it never landed. The next day Freddy went back to the candy shop. A sign out front said it was closed. The day after that it was still closed.

The following day the store was open. Freddy walked in. Mr. LaBarbara from the bank was working behind the counter. *What was Mr. LaBarbara doing there?* Freddy asked Mr. LaBarbara for a pound of sugar cubes. It had been weeks since Freddy had last had candy, and he had a lot of catching up to do. Mr. LaBarbara told him that he had recently acquired a house for free and subsequently flipped his old one. With the proceeds he had purchased the candy store, took home all the candy, and reopened it as a vegetable shop. Freddy had never eaten a vegetable, so he told Mr. LaBarbara to give him a pound of whatever tasted most like candy. Mr. LaBarbara gave Freddy a bag of radish. Freddy went outside and took a bite of a radish. He spat it out. It tasted nothing like candy. He chucked the bag at a moving car and walked home.

Freddy scoured the town for candy. There was none to be found. The Dare Street candy shop was the only candy source in town. Freddy was bewildered. He had made a wish for unlimited candy, and it seemed he was not getting any candy at all. *What went wrong? Was it because there was taffy on the quarter?* Regardless of the reason, Freddy found himself on an all-vegetable diet. And one day, while biting into a stock of broccoli he remembered what the Indian at the well had told them. It was then that Freddy realized that the well was not a wishing well at all, at least not in the traditional understanding of one.

This was a *bad* wishing well.

Truman was in the emergency room at the hospital. He had been beaten up by a gang of women. As he lay there recovering, he thought of the Indian's words on the hill. It was then that Truman made a realization: it was a *bad* wishing well.

Bud and his wife huddled in their cardboard box shivering. It had snowed six feet that evening and was not about to let up. He thought of what the Indian had said on Halloween night. It was then that Bud made a realization of his own: it was a *bad* wishing well.

They met at the Mettaquem Casino. Bud suggested they sit at the bar because he had no money for the slots. Truman had a black-eye and walked with crutches. Bud had frost-bite and was wearing rags. Freddy chewed on a carrot stick and had lost much weight. Bud and

Truman drank beer. Freddy requested soda, as it was the liquid most similar to candy. The bartender said they were out of soda. He offered Freddy vegetable juice.

"I think we all realize now," said Truman, sipping his beer, "that that was no ordinary wishing well that we cast our coins upon."

"It's a bad wishing well," confirmed Freddy.

"It is indeed," said Truman. "In fact, not only is this wishing well bad, it seems to grant you the *opposite* of whatever you wished for."

"I think it has something to do with that crow," said Bud. "What'd that Indian call it?"

"'Croatoan,'" answered Freddy, remembering the mysterious word carved on a fence post.

"Regardless," said Truman, "what do we do about this?"

Bud and Freddy were stumped.

The casino owner Sitting Crow walked by, saying, "Why don't you knuckleheads just make new wishes?"

"Will that work?" asked Bud.

"Why are you bothering me with this?" answered Sitting Crow. "We have a prime rib special at our lunch buffet." He walked away.

Truman considered Sitting Crow's suggestion. He shrugged. "It's worth a try."

"I say we go back to that well, and do what Sitting Crow says," said Bud. "We'll try some new wishes—*opposite* wishes. I'll wish for no money, you'll wish for no love, and the kid will wish for no candy. That oughta reverse these bad tidings."

"When do we do this?" asked Freddy, chewing on an asparagus stick. "I don't know how much longer I can go eating this crap."

"And I don't know how much longer my cardboard box is going to hold up," said Bud. "It's starting to get soggy with snow. Beatrice is getting pissed."

"And I don't know if I'll be able to survive this aching in my heart," added Truman. "We will go tonight."

And the others agreed.

They retraced the route they had taken Halloween night. A fresh sheet of snow blanketed the ground and tree branches. The air was cold, and they shivered as they walked. They went single-file up the hill, the moon guiding them. Bud first, Freddy second, Truman, who was on crutches, was last. The summit was near. Bud parted the branches of the poplar tree... and there was no well. No well, no Indian, no crow—just the headwaters of a stream seeping from the ground.

"What now?" asked Bud.

Truman rested his head on a crutch, exhausted. He looked around. "We search the woods."

"For what?" asked Bud.

"I don't know. For clues, I think. We need to know those other verses of that rhyme." Truman looked at Freddy. Freddy nodded, gnawing on a beet.

The trio went back down the hill, following the stream. They reached the bottom and scoured the surrounding woods. Branches and shrubbery attacked their flesh, inflaming Bud's frostbite and irritating Truman's bruises. Their feet were numb from the cold. The trio continued. They discovered a cave buried in the hillside. They entered. The glow of a fire flickered deep in the cave. An old woman hovered over a bubbling cauldron.

Without looking up, she said, "Sit down. Please." The trio huddled on the ground by the fire, warming themselves.

"Would you gentleman like something to eat?"

"Candy," Freddy said.

The old lady smiled, knowingly. "I can offer you Brussels sprouts." She dipped a ladle into the cauldron, scooping a serving of the vegetables. Freddy opened his hands, accepting the offer begrudgingly. He ate.

"Have you come for the wishing well?" she asked.

"We have," said Truman, perking up. "What can you tell us about it?"

The old woman considered the question. "Let me ask you," she said, "what do *you* know of it?"

"Well," said Truman, "the wishing well is something we've heard rumors of since we were children. There's this... nursery rhyme everybody knows. But they say it's missing a verse, maybe two. Anyway, Bud, the kid, and I found the well a little while back. It was on a hill above the stream, just like the rhyme said. An Indian was up there. He tried to stop us. We ignored him and made our wishes. I wished for love, Bud wished for money, and the kid wished for candy.

But we didn't get any of those things. In fact, our lives have been going up in smoke ever since. We have since returned to the well's location, but it is no longer there."

"When did you find the well originally?"

"It was Halloween night."

The old lady nodded, confirming something in her mind. "The well," she said, "is very old. Older than you, older than the colonies, older than most of the trees. It's cursed of course, but you know that by now. If I remember correctly, on All Hallow's Eve many years ago, an Indian chief's pet bird drowned in that well."

"Croatoan?" asked Freddy.

"That's the one," said the old lady. "He loved that bird. Anyway, the Indian chief cursed the well and the bird's ghost now haunts it. Since then the other Indians have learned to stay away from it. They guard it. You say you know a verse to the Indian ode. Tell me, which verse do you know?"

Freddy spoke.

"'For wishes to fulfill, just follow river's course.
Atop a lonely hill, awaits the water's source.'"

The old lady nodded.

"Are there other verses?" asked Bud.

"Oh yes," said the old lady. "You know the first verse. There are two more. Four hundred years ago, some other men entered my cave, asking about the well. I told them the first verse, the one that you know, and I also told them the second."

"What is the second?" asked Truman.

"'A single night a year, the wishing well is seen,
The fountain will appear the night of Halloween.'"

The trio considered this. It explained why the well they wished upon was no longer there.

The old lady continued. "I did not offer those other men the third verse, the most important one. There have been others in my cave since then. I have told no one the final verse. Instead, I have watched them *live* it, as I watch you gentlemen live it now. You are very fortunate to have only wished for love, money, and candy. You should see what happens to those that wish for something like eternal life... But tell me, what do you intend to do when you stand before the well again? ... Assuming of course that you can last until the next All Hallow's Eve..."

"We plan to make new wishes," said Truman. "*Opposite* wishes. We want to counter the spell... Please, tell us... What is the final verse?"

The old lady looked at the boy. She paused, then spoke.

"'All seekers heed the spell of ancient water's curse,
All wishes to the well are granted in reverse.'"

Truman and Bud hung their heads. Freddy chewed nervously on the vegetables. The old lady leaned back, studying them. Freddy asked, "What does all this mean?"

"It means it's true that this is a bad wishing well, just like that Indian said," answered Truman. "It also means you'll be eating vegetables for a while. We have a lot of surviving to do."

It was December when they entered the witch's cave. The next Halloween would be a long ways away.

Ten months is a long time.

Truman spent much of that period in the confines of hospital rooms and jail cells. He continued to pester Sally at the casino. He asked her out on dates almost daily. Of course, Truman was arrested on every one of these attempts for violating the restraining order that Sally had placed on him. Women continued to assault him openly on the street. For ten months Truman traversed in a rotation of canes, crutches, and wheelchairs.

Many nights, Truman stood outside Sally's house watching her. It was Bud's old house of course, and she lived there with her husband Mr. LaBarbara and her one-legged mother. Truman was still in love with Sally, and he counted the days until Halloween.

Bud spent his days at the accounting firm in which he still worked, and his nights in the cardboard box with Beatrice under the bridge. It had been a rough winter, and Beatrice was beginning to get fed up. Bud kept trying to save money, but terrible things continued to happen to his paychecks. One week, his boss misspelled Bud's name on the check, and Mr. LaBarbara at the bank refused to deposit it. Another week, Bud forgot to endorse the check, and Mr. LaBarbara was forced to void and shred it. Also, there was this crow that kept snatching checks out of Bud's hands on his walks to the bank. Bud was seriously considering signing up for direct-deposit. His cardboard box was beginning to get holes in it.

Most nights, Bud stood outside Mr. LaBarbara's house, which of course used to belong to him. Mr. LaBarbara and his wife Sally had added a third and fourth story to the home, as well as a hot tub in the back yard. Sally's one-legged mother would often take evening soaks in the tub to soothe her remaining limb. Bud still yearned for money and a home not made of paper. He counted the days until Halloween.

Freddy spent his days at Manteo Elementary. He turned ten years old, and began the fourth grade. Ms. Agnes was no longer Freddy's teacher. Sometimes he walked by her third-grade classroom, overhearing her telling the new students about the mysteries of Roanoke and the wonders of magic wishing wells. Freddy lost a significant amount of weight due to his all-vegetable diet. The chubby kid was now lean and trim. He was also the fastest runner in class. The girls began to notice Freddy. He went through multiple girlfriends the summer between the third and fourth grades. It was a miserable period. Freddy thought girls were boring, but without candy, dating was the only option available to him.

Most nights, Freddy stood outside Mr. LaBarbara's new house. Freddy watched Mr. LaBarbara and his wife and her one-legged mother eat candy. The candy, of course, came from the old Dare Street candy shop that Mr. LaBarbara had purchased and turned into a vegetable store.

Freddy longed for candy. He despised vegetables and his new trim physique, as well as the attention from girls with which this came. He counted the days until Halloween.

The afternoon sun shined brightly through the blinds of the hospital room. Truman had just awoken from his coma. A variety of tubes snaked out of different parts of his body. A machine by the bed beeped steadily. Truman had been roughed up by a posse of teenage girls in an alleyway. He stretched his aching limbs in the bed. He looked at the calendar. It was October Thirty-First, Halloween! Truman rang for the nurse.

The nurse came, accompanied by the doctor. The nurse, a female, glared at Truman.

"When can I check out of here?" Truman asked the doctor.

"That remains to be seen," said the physician. "You'll need a few more surgeries. Your injuries are quite severe."

"How about today?"

"That's out of the question. Your condition is highly unstable. In all seriousness, I'm not sure if you're going to make it." The doctor left the room.

"Can I have some cookies?" Truman asked the nurse. The nurse spat on him and left the room.

When the door shut, Truman tore the tubes out of his body. The beeping machine went berserk. He got up from the bed. His legs felt weak. He pulled up the blinds and looked out the window. It appeared he was on the third floor. A drainage pipe by the window shot down to the street. Truman saw a wheelchair sitting in the corner of the room. He grabbed the wheelchair and flung it through the window. The glass shattered everywhere. The emergency alert siren sounded off. Truman leaned out the window and wrapped his hands around the drainage pipe. He slid down to the street, and hopped into the wheelchair.

He had to get to that wishing well.

Bud awoke from his afternoon nap in the cardboard box. His boss had forgotten to pay him again that week. Beatrice snored beside Bud in the box. She was still mad at him for their lack of money. Their box had been without a roof for some time. One of the walls was getting flimsy. A leaf trickled down, landing on Bud's face. He held the leaf, studying it. Falling leaves could only mean one thing. It was autumn—the harvest was in!

He called out to the other guy who lived in a box by the bridge. "Hey man, what day is it?"

The other guy checked the calendar markings he had made on his box. "It's October Thirty-First."

It was Halloween! Bud crawled out of his box and stretched. Dusk was approaching. He had to get to that wishing well.

Freddy was bored in class. He nibbled on a bowl of peas. His girlfriend sat in the seat next to him. She sipped on a coffee beverage. A pumpkin spice scent wafted over to Freddy. *Pumpkin spice?* Freddy knew that could only mean one thing. It was October. He turned to the classroom calendar hanging on the wall. It was October Thirty-First, Halloween!

When school ended, Freddy rushed out of the classroom. His girlfriend stopped him. "How about a romantic walk on the beach tonight?" she suggested, batting her eyelids.

"No thanks."

"But if we go to the beach, I just might hold your hand."

"Not interested," said Freddy. "Also, I'm breaking up with you."

He dropped his bowl of peas in a trash can. He ran off in the direction of the woods. He had to get to that wishing well.

They met at Fort Raleigh at the edge of the forest. It was dusk. Bud pushed Truman's wheelchair. Freddy carried Truman's crutches. They began their trek through the woods. Their journey was silent and without confusion. They knew precisely how to arrive at their destination. The boys reached the stream at the base of the hill. It was night now. The moon blazed above them. A wolf howled in the distance. A bat flapped from one tree to the next. Truman left his wheelchair at the hill's base. Freddy handed him the crutches. They went up slowly.

They were near the peak. Freddy parted the branches of the poplar tree... and the wishing well waited for them in the glowing moonlight. The trio approached the well. Truman did not hesitate dispersing the new coins. They were about to make their new wishes.

"Halt!" someone shouted behind them. The boys turned. The Indian once again stepped from out of the shrubbery. Croatoan sat on his shoulder. "What are your intentions with well?"

"We want to make new wishes with different coins," answered Truman. "We want to reverse the spell. I'll wish for no love, Bud will wish for no money, and the kid will wish for no candy."

"Won't work," said the Indian. The crow squawked. "Silence, Croatoan!"

"Why won't it work?" said Truman.

"Can't change spell with different coins. Must retrieve *old* coins. Then make new wishes." The Indian turned, walking back to the thicket. Croatoan flew off in the night, its screeching echoing throughout the forest.

"How do we get our old coins back?" asked Bud to the group.

Freddy peered down into the well. He looked at Truman's crutches. Truman understood. He handed Bud a crutch. Freddy grabbed the other end. Bud lowered Freddy down into the well. They were very fortunate that Freddy had lost so much weight, otherwise Bud would not have been able to hold him. Freddy reached the water. He let go of the crutch. The water he floated in was startlingly cold. Freddy looked up. Bud and Truman watched from the rim of the well, their faces silhouetted by the moon above them.

Freddy took a deep breath and went below the water's surface. The moon allowed just enough light for him to see. He reached the bottom of the well. There were many coins resting on the floor. Some were new, others were old, and many were of denominations that Freddy did not understand. *So many lives ruined,* he thought. Freddy found his old quarter. It was still covered in taffy. He put it in his pocket. Truman's Susan B. Anthony dollar stood out among the other coins. Freddy grabbed it. There was only one penny in the well. Freddy knew it must be Bud's.

He was about to swim up when a particular coin caught his eye. Freddy picked it up, studying it. The coin was very old and corroded. It appeared to be an old English shilling. Queen Elizabeth's face was on it. Freddy was reminded of Ms. Agnes' class discussions. He thought about her friends from the Roanoke Archaeological and Historical Society. They were probably at Ms. Agnes' home at this very moment exchanging their funny theories. Freddy let the coin drop from his hand. It floated to the bottom of the well. He swam up.

He grabbed the crutch. Bud pulled him up. Freddy shivered in the moonlight. Bud handed him one of his rags with which to get warm. It was time to make their wishes. Freddy dispersed the coins. They stood around the well, their coins in their hands.

"I wish for no love!" shouted Truman. "I want all women to hate me, especially Sally!"

"I wish for no money!" shouted Bud. "I want to live in that box forever!"

"And I wish for no candy!" shouted Freddy. "I want to eat only vegetables!"

The forest came alive. Wolves howled. Owls hooted. Bats flapped. Crows squawked. The wind raged. The boys exchanged glances. Truman nodded. They dropped their coins simultaneously. The wind stopped, and the sounds of the forest ceased.

"Now let's get the hell out of here," said Truman. Bud and Freddy did not argue.

The boys were cheerful coming down the mountain. Truman ditched the crutches. His legs were already feeling better. Just then, his cell phone chirped. It was a text message from Sally. It said, "How about a date tonight, stud?"

Bud was merry, but chilly coming down the hill. His nose was stuffed. He reached into his pocket for a tissue. He grabbed one. He was about to blow his nose into it when he realized it was a hundred dollar bill.

Freddy, soaking wet, was also cold. He trudged down the hill hunched over. On the ground an object glowed, reflecting the moonlight. Freddy reached down to grab it. It was a chocolate bar. He tore the wrapper and took a bite.

The boys reached the bottom of the hill. They would soon be back in town to start their new lives. Truman planned to head straight to the casino. Serving cocktails in the casino was a beautiful woman with whom he would like to get acquainted. Bud would walk directly to Beatrice and the box. Tonight they would be staying at the fanciest hotel in town. The following day they would purchase a mansion. Freddy had a lot of trick-or-treating to do. His first stop would be Ms. Agnes' house. He had a story or two for her and her society friends.

The three boys walked toward the glowing lights of town.

Passing by them, unseen in the darkness, was Mr. LaBarbara, the banker/ vegetable proprietor. He had grown up in Roanoke, and had always heard of a magic wishing well. His old neighbor Ms. Agnes and her society friends spoke of it constantly. Like all Roanokers, Mr. LaBarbara had grown up hearing about a nursery rhyme.

For wishes to fulfill, just follow river's course,
Atop a lonely hill, awaits the water's source.

In his search for the river, Mr. LaBarbara had gotten lost. He came across an old woman in a cave making a stew. She informed him that he was missing a verse. Mr. LaBarbara was in luck. Apparently, the wishing well only came out on Halloween!

Mr. LaBarbara left the cave and found a stream. It was at the base of a hill. He looked up. The water seemed to be coming from the summit. The wishing well must be there. A crow with orange eyes sat on a tree branch, watching him. Mr. LaBarbara reached into his pocket. He withdrew several rolls of quarters. It was one of the perks of working at a bank. He began to climb the hill.

He had a lot of wishes to make.

Milltree Guest House

Marsha Webb

It had been a really tiring day. John had not realised how long it was going to take him to drive between the farms. On the map the journey looked straight forward but in real life the narrow, twisted lanes had to be handled with care. Cattle, other vehicles and the weather all slowed him down. John was an agricultural salesman and he was seeing seven farms in the area, four today and three tomorrow. He had booked a little guesthouse roughly half way between his last farm today and his first appointment tomorrow.

The rain lashed down, his wiper speed was on maximum yet he still struggled to see out. The windscreen misted up continually, the lanes were pitch black, there were no street lights on these country roads. The roads were twisted and windy with sudden sharp bends, his progress was very slow, he was tired and hungry. His Sat Nav had stopped working due to lack of signal some time ago and he was starting to face the real threat that he might have to spend the night in his car with nothing to eat or drink. As he braked to navigate a steep hill he saw the sign, "Milltree Guest House". He turned with relief up the gravelly drive and heard the satisfying crunch under his tires.

The long driveway was framed by trees either side, shivering in the bitter wind. When he reached the end, the imposing house was not a welcoming sight. John shivered involuntarily, it looked creepy. The huge wooden door reminded him of an entrance in an old fashioned horror movie. The turrets at the top of the house looked like they could be small dungeons used to chain long forgotten prisoners. John chided himself, he was being stupid, it was only for one night and he was tired and hungry. He checked his watch. Nine thirty. He had told the receptionist he would be there by seven.

He ran across the carpark through the cascading rain, although only a short run he felt soaked through, drops sneaked down his neck and ran off his nose. He knocked loudly on the door with the brass knocker. No answer, he knocked again and it was opened by a thin well-dressed woman in her sixties.

"Mr Griffiths?" she enquired, peering at him "I was expecting you at seven".

"I am so sorry" John replied, fidgeting with his bag on the threshold.

She moved aside to let him in. "Kitchen is closed now, you will not get a hot meal, I made you some beef sandwiches though if you want them."

"Oh yes please" John said, grateful he would eat at all tonight.

She went to retrieve them and he had a chance to look around. The place looked like it was once grand, almost regal, but had sadly been left to decay and ruin. The wallpaper was faded and dated; there was thick dust on the shelves housing trinkets of a by gone era. The lights were very dim; just two small wall lights with dark red lampshades provided the light for the hall and reception area. The grandfather clock ticked loudly from the corner like a scolding headmaster. There was a damp musty smell in the air. He felt a cold breeze on his neck like a whisper from the dead. He turned around sharply.

"Here you go" The woman's voice broke the tension. She handed him the sandwiches, cling filmed on a white plate. "You can take them up to your room". She checked him in, "You are in room six on the first floor and the bathroom is at the far end of the corridor. Enjoy your stay". She handed him a cold metal key.

He walked up the creaky stairs, the carpets looked a wine colour but with the thick layer of undisturbed dust it was difficult to tell. The wall lights on the stairs dimly illuminated the paintings of people from long ago, history echoed within their faces. Their eyes watched his slow, careful assent to the first floor. He found the bathroom first, then made his way to his bedroom. The room was basic, just a bed, wardrobe and bedside table, no television, no Wi-Fi or phone signal. John sat down on the hand embroidered, pink bed cover, tiny particles of dust were launched into the air and the musty smell encircled his nostrils. He ate his sandwich to the drumming of the heavy rain then got into bed. He started to doze off when he was woken by doors slamming and people laughing and talking, *another group must have arrived late*, he thought. They took a while to settle, he checked his watch it was only eleven o'clock. He dozed again and awoke to the sound of heavy footsteps outside his door. It was going to be one of those nights.

Now he was awake John needed the toilet. He put on his dressing gown and opened his door. At that point the bright flash of lightning lit up the whole of the corridor and he saw an old man hunched over with silver grey hair, in his slippers shuffling towards the bathroom. He shut his door again, the explosive crack of the thunder made him jump. He sat on his bed watching the rain through the window for ten minutes to give the old gentleman time to finish. He peered out of his door just as the old man was passing his room and going into the room next door.

"Evening" John said, being polite. The man didn't respond. Maybe he was deaf. John pulled the bathroom light switch but no light came on. *Great, a power cut*. He felt his way to the toilet and began urinating when another blaze of lightning lit up the bathroom. He noticed a shadow behind him and he turned quickly, there was a lady sitting on the side of the bath.

He screamed "What are you doing in here? Why didn't you say anything when I came in?" He angled his body away from her. No answer, and the thunder clapped right above the house. Another flash of lightning, she was gone, had she rushed out in distress? He saw the silhouette of the shower cap, had he imagined it, was it just a trick of the light?

He moved quickly back to his room. He saw the old man walking slowly down the stairs with his head bowed, where was he going now, it was all shut up down there? John shut his door and tried to sleep, it was so noisy. The laughing, door slamming and footsteps continued into the early hours. Eventually he fell asleep about five am. At seven o'clock a car door slamming woke him with a jolt. He looked out of his window which was overlooking the car park and watched the woman who had greeted him last night walk towards the house with a shopping bag in her hand. His car was the only other one in the carpark.

He was awake now, so he took his washbag towards the bathroom. He knocked on the door and shouted "Anybody in here?" He was not going to make the same mistake as last night. He locked himself in and had a tepid shower whist battling with the temperamental plumbing work. The groaning and bangs of the pipework must have woken everyone in the house up. Still, they kept him awake most of the night so he didn't feel too guilty.

He walked into the breakfast room and the lady of the house greeted him wearing a chef's apron over her smart clothing.

"Tea or coffee?"

"Coffee please. White, two sugars."

"Full English breakfast?"

"Yes please I'm starving" John`s stomach rumbled on cue.

"Help yourself to toast, cereal and fruit juice."

She retreated again into the kitchen. John looked around; he had the whole breakfast room to himself, the other tables empty and forlorn. The orange tablecloths were clean but faded, the dark red wallpaper, the same as the hall made the room look small and dated. There was a sad, dusty plastic flower in a thin vase on each table. He certainly would not be giving this place a five star review on TripAdvisor.

His breakfast was set beside him, it looked delicious. The woman took off her apron,

"Did you sleep well?"

"It was a bit noisy, to be honest."

Her face furrowed in confusion.

"How many guests are here at the moment?" he enquired between mouthfuls of juicy sausages and perfectly cooked eggs.

"Just you" she replied, folding her apron and walking back to the kitchen.

Fly Babies

Gayle Fidler

The Autumn equinox, this is the day that the festivities start. The equinox marks the end of Summer and beginning of Autumn. Day and night of equal length. A magical celebration, a time to give thanks for all that has been received, as we begin to prepare for the darkness of the coming days.

I cannot say how long our family has celebrated these changes in the seasons. My Grandmother, Lilly was her name, would sit me on her knee in front of the fire when I was a small child. Lilly would stare into the flames, as she jogged me slowly up and down. She would tell me stories of gathering fruit, nuts and leaves with her own Grandmother, many, many years before. The following day she would take me into the woods, basket in hand and we would continue the tradition. Coming home carrying a basket laden with colour. Greens and browns, yellows and reds. Shades of foraged Autumn to decorate the house.

Lilly was a hundred and three when she died, peacefully in her own bed. The day after she passed, I helped my mother and my aunts. We laid her out in her sitting room. We washed her, brushed her hair and dressed her in her favourite black lace gown. I remember gazing down at her, marvelling at how peaceful she looked. I even thought I saw her smile up at me, her lips twitched ever so slightly upwards and all was right with the world. My own daughter, Scarlett, was five years old at the time. Lilly had been teaching her how to make corn dollies to honour the cycle of birth, death and rebirth.

Scarlett came into the room the day we laid her out. She had made the most beautifully woven pieces of corn, which she lovingly tucked between her Great Grandmothers' hands. Family traditions are such an important part of life. Our children are brought up to honour the dead, not to be afraid or sad.

Scarlett is sixteen now, she has grown into the most magnificent young woman, although still with a child like innocence about her. I look forward to the adventures and opportunities that lie ahead of her. As a mother, I have taught her well. A strong woman raised by generations of strong women.

As tradition dictates, now that my parents are elderly and Lilly has passed, they have moved into her rooms. One day we will lay my mother out in the same sitting room. I hope that on that day I will see her smiling too

Evening is falling, in the garden a fire is burning. The smoke rises and dances in the autumn breeze. Within the house, candles are lit. The flames flicker across the ancient stone walls, casting shadows which create pockets of darkness. It is living art, a work of beauty. I once had an interior designer friend over for tea. She suggested we should plaster the whole house. Her rationale was that it would make the rooms appear warmer and easier on the eye. I laughed at her. There is nothing easier on the eye than ancient stones, each one has a story to tell if you know how to listen. I never invited her to tea again.

My extended family all live in the house. It is not cramped; the house is far bigger than we are. There is plenty of room for more.

The sun sets and we gather in the dining room for a feast. Scarlett has spent the day in the woods foraging with Chloe, her younger niece. They have come home with a most magnificent haul and decorated the downstairs rooms with all manner of beautiful colours. It makes me breathless to look at it.

Tonight, we dine on beef served rare and cut from one of our own cows. I chose her especially for this meal, such a beauty she was. A Hereford that Scarlett named Twiggy, ironic really, looking at the amount of meat that sits on the platter. The meal is accompanied with potatoes, carrots, leeks, parsnips and cauliflower. Seasoned with herbs picked from our gardens. My husband has dusted off a few bottles of fine wine from the cellar. Before we married, he did not have a nose for wine. My father has taught him well.

The dining table is large enough for all the family, but nowhere near big enough to fill the dining room. One of the most expansive rooms in the house, Lilly always loved this room, once she told me the tale of my Grandfather proposing to her at this very table. He presented her with the most exquisite blue sapphire engagement ring. My mother keeps it in her jewellery box, one day it will pass to me, then to Scarlett.

The evening rolls on, outside the fire is kept burning. Occasionally, my husband or one of my nephews will go out to tend to it. Their job is to keep it burning over the weeks that follow. The fire outside must burn continuously until the day after our next great feast. It is needed to light the way. The fire will burn brightly in our garden, it guides those that are lost, safely home.

We eat, we drink, we laugh, we reminisce. We tell stories only a family would find amusing. The time when Uncle Thomas fell asleep on an ant nest. The time when my sister Alice was thrown from her pony into the duck pond.

Most importantly of all, we give thanks. Thanks for all that we have, and all that has been in the year that has passed. Thanks for a wonderful family, good fortune, our health, food on the table and a beautiful home.

Chloe tells us that she has named one of our pigs Pumpkin. She tries to stifle her giggles, as she admits to sneaking him extra food to make him super fat.

Chloe is ten now, for the past few years she has chosen the pig that we will eat at the next great family feast. Chloe has started her own little tradition of announcing the pigs name at the equinox dinner. For the next month she will regale us with tales of her and Pumpkin, Chloe is just the sweetest little thing. My sister and I have joked recently, that it will not be long until the little girl is slaughtering the swine herself!

By eleven all the children are tucked up asleep in their beds. Every year, they are adamant that they will make it past midnight, but they never do. The day of Autumn equinox is such a busy one, little legs are so easily tired out.

The adults retire to the drawing room. My husband spends the rest of the evening playing chess with my father. They are a fiercely competitive pair, tempers flare before the night is out. This is not an unusual occurrence; the rest of the family ignore the cross exchanges. We are used to it; it has become another family tradition.

We once lost an ancestor to a game of chess; things became so heated his brother shot him in the leg with a pistol. Lilly would repeatedly tell us the tale whenever she was served rice at dinner. The unfortunate man was adamant it was just a scratch and refused to clean the wound. It became so infected that my great aunt had to have him tied to the bed and remove maggots with a pair of tweezers. He did not last long after that, dying, delirious from infection in the room which Scarlett now sleeps in.

When she was a small girl, Scarlett christened the room her "little fly trap". The maggot story used to make her laugh. Lilly would pick pieces of rice from her plate and flick them at Scarlett, who would pop them into her mouth, giggling and singing about eating fly babies. This is how she learnt to count.

"One fly baby from Uncle Fred's leg.

Two fly babies, he is nearly dead.

Three fly babies, there will be more.

Four fly babies, buzzing at the door."

There is one last tradition to uphold before we retire to bed. Each family member pours themselves a glass from the decanter that now sits on the hall stand by the front door. The glasses are laid out in advance. We always put out extra just in case the children manage to join us.

This decanter is only used for the equinox. It has been brought out from Lilly's' room. My mother has washed and polished it for the occasion. The crystal sparkles in the hall light, the liquid inside, a smooth, dark, rich red. It looks so delicious. A black and white photo of Lilly on her wedding day sits next to the decanter, she looks so beautiful. The most perfect blushing bride, so young and full of life.

We take our glasses outside to the fire. We stand for a moment, taking in the beauty of the sunrise accompanied by glowing embers of the fire. My mother raises her glass and we offer a toast "To those that have been, and to those that are to come". My husband throws more logs on the fire, to keep it going until we awake. We embrace, then all head to our respective rooms. The Autumn equinox may be over for another year, but the best is yet to come.

The weeks that follow are spent giddy with anticipation. The house is cleaned thoroughly from top to bottom. Traditionally a lot of families have a spring clean. We have an autumn one. Everything must look perfect for our next big celebration. Samhain, the beginning of winter. The day traditionally when herds of cattle would be driven down from the hills. Also, the day when the dead are welcomed back.

Samhain celebrations begin at sunrise. The children excitedly collect windfallen apples from the orchard, throwing rotten ones at each other, howling with laughter as the fruit bounces off legs and backs. Some are squashy and disintegrate on contact, others are still hard. There will be bruises tonight no doubt.

We gather as a family for breakfast, this morning we will have scrambled eggs, served with rashers of bacon, accompanied by mushrooms from our woods. Chloe pops a slice of bacon into her mouth, and makes an oinking sound, mimicking a pig. "Is this a fat pumpkin pig?" she asks.

Her mother tells her that it is not Pumpkin, he will be eaten later. Then scolds her for talking with her mouth full. Chloe rolls her eyes at Scarlett and swallows her food with a look of disappointment on her face.

Outside, there is a light drizzle and a breeze which rattles the windowpanes. The rest of the morning is spent mostly indoors. I sit by the fire in the kitchen reading a book, while my mother prepares vegetables. I offer to help, but she turns me down, telling me to make the most of my time while the children are quiet.

The children are too quiet, they have not been seen since breakfast. I always worry when this happens. What mischief are they getting into?

Lunchtime comes and goes; we eat onion soup with homemade bread served at the kitchen table. The children still have not joined us. Mother says not to worry, she will leave their soup to keep warm on the stove. Children always come home when they are hungry.

Evening begins to draw in, the cooking smells coming from the kitchen are wonderful. Pumpkin has been roasting all day. My mouth waters as I imagine the flesh falling away in strips as the carving knife slices effortlessly through it. Still no sign of the children, the house feels silent. We go and dress for dinner.

In the dining room, mother remarks on the empty seats at the table. My husband shrugs his shoulders and takes a sip of wine. He may not be worried, but I am starting to feel uneasy. Whatever capers they have been into during the day, they should be here by now. As the oldest, Scarlett is aware of what time dinner is served. Chloe would not want to miss out on the serving of her big, fat Pumpkin either.

The Grandfather clock in the hall chimes seven times. We really must begin dinner, or we will be late for the celebrations.

I pick up my knife and fork, and nervously pick at my starter. Onion and goats cheese tarts, Lilly's favourite. I have lost my appetite; I glance at my mother, but she seems unconcerned. I can hear the clock ticking in the hall. The rhythm beats in my head.

One fly baby, Scarlett's gone.
Two fly babies, no children here.

I have listened to that clock my entire life, but it has never seemed as loud as it does now.

Three fly babies, wherever can they be?

Four fly babies, they all disappear.

Beads of sweat have formed on my brow. I use my napkin to dab them away. The clock chimes once, half past the hour. My husband is staring at the window, something has caught his eye. I turn my head to look and then I see it too. Complete darkness, the garden fire no longer burns.

That is when the door to the dining room opens and the children step inside. The four of them. Scarlett at the front, my two nephews, and little Chloe at the back. I should feel relief, but I do not. I feel dread and disappointment, tinged with anger. My mother has gone white, I fear she may faint.

The children stand in a line and smile at us. They are expecting a reward for their big achievement.

"What have you done?" My younger sister squeals at them. She always had a squeaky, irritating voice. Tonight, it has become more so.

A fly lands on the dining table.

Scarlett is wearing a wedding gown. She has put on a little make up and twisted her hair up into a bun. On her wedding finger is Lilly's engagement ring. Cradled in her arms is a white knitted blanket, it is tucked in, swaddling the shape of a baby. The other three children carry similar shaped bundles.

"We brought them back," Chloe excitedly announces, "They wanted to see Pumpkin, I told them all about him."

My husband swats away another insect.

I walk over to Scarlett and peer down at the lifeless shape in her arms. I peel back the blanket. A fly escapes. My daughter is not cradling a human child, instead she holds a dead rabbit, it no longer has a head. In its place is a turnip, with a face carved into it.

Four fly babies all in a row.

"Every year, you honour them," Scarlett said. I had no idea my daughter could talk in such an authoritative tone. "You feast for a month, you keep the fires lit to guide them home, but every year, they get here and you never open the door. Today, we did. We found a way to let them in from the cold. The corn dollies kept their spirits safe. They rest in these babies now."

I take the rabbit bundle gently from Scarlett's arms and gaze down into the hollows of the turnip face. A fly crawls from the eye socket and the mouth smiles up at me.

Small World

H. K. Hillman

One rose early, as every morning, and checked the food cupboard. It had the day's food as always. She lifted the bags and took them to the kitchen where she placed the chilled food in the fridge and the rest in the cupboard. The toiletries she left on the table. They would be dispersed to the bathrooms later.

The others stirred. She heard them rising from their beds, heard them in their bathrooms and thought about Three. Three was the one she wanted as a mate but she knew Four liked him too. Two was, well, a bit weird. He spent too long thinking and thinking, as everyone knew, only led to problems.

She walked into the hallway towards the living room and this morning, as every morning, her gaze drifted to the dusty hazmat suits hanging beside The Door. The door to Outside. Where there was nothing but death. They had worn those suits many years before, as had their guides, before they had entered the safe place where they now lived. Just children at that time. The suits certainly wouldn't fit them now.

The guides had told them they were all that was left. All of humanity in these last four. Outside was certain death, and they must stay safe in these few rooms to keep humanity alive. One shivered and pushed open the door to the living room.

To her surprise, Two was already there. Sat on the sofa, leaning forward, elbows on the coffee table, hands over his face. This was out of sequence. It was wrong. It was not how the day progressed. He should be still in his bathroom. One stood in shock, staring.

Finally, Two lowered his hands and smiled a crooked smile at her. "Did I surprise you, One? Don't I always do that?" He burst into bitter-sounding laughter. "Oh I have so much more to surprise you with today."

"Why are you up so early? You are out of sequence. Are you trying to ruin the day?" One's lip trembled. This was outside her experience and she didn't know what, if anything, she should do.

"I'm not up early. I'm up late. I couldn't sleep." Two rubbed at his face. "I'm greasy. I'll need a shower soon."

One's legs trembled. Scared she might fall, she moved to sit opposite Two. "What have you done? You are far out of sequence. You risk killing us all with your non-compliance."

"Nothing is going to kill us, and we are not the last humans." Two let his head rest in his hands. "I'm not sure you are ready for this, heck I'm not sure I am."

"Explain. Quickly." One looked over her shoulder. Three and Four would be looking for breakfast soon. She needed to quell this lunacy before they were infected.

"I hacked into Parent's core processors last night. I went past the firewall."

"What!" One reacted as if he had hacked into the mind of God, and perhaps, in this world, he had.

"I read something. About monkeys." Two blew a long breath. "Something disturbing. And a lot more."

"You even being here is disturbing." One clenched her fists and lifted them to her pinched face. "This is all wrong. This is not how the day goes."

"That's the thing. It's exactly the same day, every day, You, Three and Four just accept it, every day and never question anything. I'm the one who asked the question."

"What question?"

Two lifted his eyebrows. "Why are we here?"

One shook her head. "You know why. Outside is dead. We have to stay here until it's safe to go out and repopulate the planet. It's important. Otherwise humanity is finished."

"Did it never occur to you to wonder," Two spoke quietly, his eyes downcast, "that if everyone outside is dead, who is telling us the news? Or who taught our lessons as we grew up?" He looked up and sighed. "Who sends us food and supplies? Why does the electricity and water still work? How does any of this happen if there is nobody to make it happen?"

"Automated systems, silly." Four entered the room, her long hair swaying around her waist. "Come on, Two, enough with the tinfoil hat stuff."

Two shook his head. "Automated systems still need maintenance and power. And fresh food needs someone to grow it, pick it and deliver it. How is that happening if everyone is dead?"

Four's smile faltered. "It… just is. Look, I don't want to have to think about it. We're safe in here and we could be happy too if you'd stop all this nonsense."

One put her face in her hands, trying to stop the thoughts Two had started in her head.

"What's for breakfast?" Three strode through the door, paused to take in the scene and narrowed his eyes. "Have you been scaring the girls with your mad ideas again, Two?"

"Didn't we have names once? When we were small?" Two threw his arms in the air and stood. He strode to the television. "Now we just have numbers." He toyed with the television controls. His voice shook. "I can't remember my name. Can any of you?"

Their silence told him their answer.

One wiped her face and took a deep breath. "Breakfast. It's already late and we can't get more out of sequence. The day will be ruined." She glared at Two. "If it isn't already."

"I'll skip breakfast." Two faced the silent television. It would come to life on its own, when it was the proper time.

"You can't!" One shouted. "You've already broken sequence so badly. No more. You will have breakfast if I have to stuff it down your throat myself."

"And I'll hold you down while she does it." There was real menace in Three's voice.

"Okay, okay." Two shook his head. "I'll just have a piece of toast."

"You will have the same as the rest of us." One jutted her lower lip. "No more deviation. We're getting back to normal."

"Normal!" Two convulsed with laughter. "You all still think this is normal? A tiny home with no windows, food and utilities arrive by magic even after however long we've been in here, and we do nothing to earn any of it? This is normal?"

"It's what we know. What we've always known." Four lifted her head. "It keeps us safe, and you are meddling with that."

"Enough. Breakfast time." One stomped off to the kitchen. With glares at Two, Three and Four followed her.

Two closed his eyes. *Monkeys*, he thought. *Will I ever get them to understand?* He followed them to the kitchen.

They ate in silence. Two resisted the urge to tell them where eggs came from or to even mention the cycles of growth of cereals and the baking of bread. He had found all this when he had broken through the firewall. It's all out there, on something called 'internet'.

After breakfast, Three put the plates into the cleaning slot. They would return, spotless, in time for lunch. Two shook his head. They never questioned that either.

In keeping with their sequence, they returned to the living room. This was the time for idle chit chat before the television gave them the day's news, then they would retire to their rooms, log into Parent and read the books or play the games it sent to their screens.

This would be Two's only chance. As it turned out, One opened the conversation for him.

"You said you had damaged Parent. You'd better not have lost my high score. I was almost through the entire game."

Three and Four gaped. "You did what?" Three looked ready to punch him.

"Relax, I didn't damage anything. I just got through the firewall and into the rest of the world." Two sighed. "And I found something we should all know."

One pursed her lips. "You said something about monkeys."

"Yes." Two licked his lips. "It's a kind of story, if you like. A story about a game."

The others leaned forward. Two smiled. Stories and games were all they had ever known in this place, so his combination caught their interest at once.

"The game involves four monkeys," he began. "These four monkeys are in a windowless enclosure, and in the middle is a tall pole with a banana on the top." He bit his lip to stop himself from telling where bananas came from. It was far too soon and it would gain nothing but sneers.

"Okay," he continued. "Monkeys like bananas so one of them tries to climb the pole to get the banana. As soon as he tries, all the monkeys get sprayed with ice cold water. Eventually another tries and they all get sprayed again. Soon they learn not to climb the pole, because that will get them an ice-cold shower."

Four sniffed. "Doesn't sound like much of a game."

"Ah," Two raised his finger. "That's just the setup. Once they stop going for the banana, you take out one of the monkeys and put in a new one. This one doesn't know about the ice showers so he goes straight for the pole with the banana. The other three beat the crap out

74

of him because they know if he climbs the pole, they all get ice cold showers. This will only happen a few times before the new monkey learns to conform. At this point the new monkey knows the pole is dangerous but doesn't know why."

"No more spraying?" Three tilted his head.

"No need. You'll soon see why." Two winked. "So you take out another of the original monkeys and put in a new one. The new one goes straight for the banana at the top of the pole and the others beat the crap out of him. Including the one who doesn't know why the pole is dangerous. Then you replace another and another until none of the monkeys in the experiment know why the pole is dangerous, just that, somehow, it is."

One frowned. "But if they aren't getting the ice bath any more, surely they can just get the banana?"

Two stretched his shoulders. He really needed some sleep and a shower but he knew One wouldn't allow it at this time. "It's learned behaviour. None of the original monkeys are in there. None of the current ones have experienced the ice-cold shower. Yet they believe the pole is dangerous to climb because they have been taught to believe. Do you see?"

"Very interesting, I'm sure, but still not much of a game." Four scratched her head. "What's the point?"

Two bit into his lower lip. It was time. "We're the monkeys. We were all taken from our parents at three years old. We were already in a lockdown, we couldn't see any other family so we were preconditioned to this. We are in an experiment."

"Oh I might have known." Three rolled his eyes. "It's more tinfoil hat crap."

Two bowed his head. "We've been conditioned for this. I've asked you if you remember the names we had before we were brought here. I doubt it because I don't. Here's more. I remember my parents screaming, me screaming, as they took me from the farm. I remember crying when they put that suit on me. I remember Mary –"

"Oh yes." Four's eyes lit up. "Mary was the one in the bubble suit who checked on us every day for a long time until she said she couldn't come any more but it was okay because we could do it ourselves now."

Silence fell. One and Three's brows furrowed. Two smiled at Four. "So you remember something. There is hope."

Three sighed and shook his head. "Okay, I'll bite. If we're in an experiment, what's the point of it? What's it supposed to prove?"

"The same as that monkey experiment." Two stared directly into Three's eyes. "You know there's instant death outside, right?"

"Of course." Three looked at Four and then One for support. "So?"

Two lowered his voice to almost a whisper. "What is it? What will kill us if we go outside?"

The silence hung heavy for a while. Four broke it. "It doesn't make sense. None of us have been replaced, like in your monkey story. We've all been in here from the beginning."

Two sniffed. "That part already happened to our parents. Our real mothers and fathers. They were so scared of something 'outside' that they couldn't put up a fight when we were taken for our own safety. They were the ones getting the metaphorical cold showers. We are the monkeys who still fear the banana and have no idea why."

One ran her hands over her face and through her hair. "You haven't answered Three's question. If we're in an experiment, what's the goal? What is it intended to prove?"

"That we, like the monkeys, can be conditioned. Controlled. We can be held in thrall by a fear even if we don't know what we are scared of. You know the mantras. Comfortable compliant conformity. When there is nowhere to hide there will be nothing to fear. Stay safe. We're being... prepared. Conditioned to some new life." Two gave a lopsided smile. "I think the experiment has been, largely, a success."

"One small detail." One leaned back in her chair. "If someone is running all this, why haven't they blocked you from accessing Parent? Why haven't they taken you out of the experiment? If you are right then surely you've just wrecked the whole thing."

Two shrugged. "I just got through last night although I've been trying for months. Maybe they haven't noticed. Maybe they haven't had time to do anything. Maybe they aren't even watching because they never thought any of us would try. Or maybe I'm wrong about all of it." He stood. "There's only one way to find out for sure."

The others followed him to The Door. Two regarded the hazmat suits and traced his finger in their dusty coating. No point even trying them, they were far too small now.

Two put his hand on the door handle. He hesitated, his eyes closed, and his head tilted back. Was it true, what he had seen? Was this a beginning or an end?

"Two. Don't." One put her hand on his arm. "Outside is death. You're right, we don't know why, but it's better to stay in here. Stay safe. We know life in here. We have our daily sequence. Our comfortable compliant conformity. Come back to it. Come back to us."

Two, eyes still shut, shook his head. "This is the test. Is the Door locked for our safety or did they rely on our fear to keep it closed?"

"Don't test it." Four's voice trembled. "You might let it in."

"She's right." Three sounded harsh. "Whatever risk you want to take, you have no right to make us take the same risk."

Two opened his eyes and stared at The Door. "Fuck it," he said, and pushed down on the handle. The door swung inwards with a screech.

Light streamed in. Two stepped through the door into light and warmth. He gasped in delight at the new air, the green around him, the blank wall of doors stretching into the distance.

"What's out there?" Four shrank back from the opening.

"Are you okay?" One had one hand on the Door.

"It's wonderful. So bright. So warm. Lots of green and lots of doors like ours." Two spread his hands, "And people. With sticks,"

There was a bang. A red mist burst from the side of Two's head and he dropped, lifeless, to the ground.

One closed the door and hung her head. "He was wrong. Death is out there, and there is no escape." She clapped her hands together. "News time and then lunch."

After lunch, the new Two was installed. After a few identically sequenced days, One, Three and Four had no idea he had not been there from the beginning.

And neither did he.

Bagboy

H. K. Hillman

"What's in the bag, kid?"

The boy set down his heavy bag and stared into the eyes of the grinning man who towered over him. This man wasn't on his list.

"The head of the last person who looked into the bag," he said.

The man laughed. "Good one, kid." He patted the boy's head and walked on.

The boy picked up his bag and continued on his way. Day faded into night and still the boy walked.

As the darkness closed in, the Halloween revelries went into full swing. A man shambled past him, his grin lopsided. "Hey, kid, whass inna bag, eh?"

The boy looked into the man's eyes. Another one who wasn't on his list. "The head of the last person who looked into the bag."

The man snorted. "Smartass kid. Fegoff." He staggered away.

The boy hefted the bag onto his shoulder and headed for the place he needed to be.

Denny fiddled with his mask. It was a pain to wear it, but wear it he must, even alone in this alleyway. It had advantages in his line of work. He took out his knife, admired its stiletto gleam in the moonlight and quickly resheathed it. This was his earner, his path to riches. So far it had made him enough to be comfortable and, he had to admit, it had provided a lot of fun. One day he would strike the mother lode.

Or rather, one night. Denny smiled behind his mask. It wasn't a great mask, it was a cheap surgical mask that Denny knew did nothing to protect him from anything. Except one thing. Identification. He chuckled at the thought that in less than a year, the police had moved from arresting someone in a mask to arresting anyone without one. Times change, and they change very fast these days.

He could have chosen one of the many colourful masks now on sale, he could have picked a mask from a film or TV character. He chose this one for a reason. Most people wore this type now, even though the younger ones had forgotten why. This was true anonymity, having the same face as everyone else. In his profession, that was an ace card.

Footsteps approached. Denny tensed and sank into the shadows, prepared to grasp the night's earnings. He should have been working with Bob but Bob had not shown up for over a week and nobody knew where he was. So, for now, Denny worked alone.

A small figure, silhouetted in street lights, stood at the end of the alley. Denny watched through narrowed eyes. The figure had a large bag, there might be something of value in it. Would that little one risk the darkness of the alley or would they chicken out and take the long way around?

There was no motion for several minutes. Denny wasn't even sure he was breathing, the anticipation was so great. The small figure sniffed the air and looked around. Maybe it was listening, gauging the alley as safe or risky.

It's safe. Denny tried to push the thought into the small figure's head. Oh, he had no belief in anything supernatural but hell, it couldn't hurt to try.

The figure took a step forward. Its head moved from side to side. Denny kept his breathing shallow and silent. *This could be a big one. The kid could be a money courier for a gang. They'd never know who took that bag of cash. Maybe it's drugs. What the hell, I know enough junkies, I could sell them. Must be something valuable, nobody else would let a kid out with a bag that big this late.*

The small figure let out a snort of breath and strode into the alley.

Denny tensed, his hand on his blade. This had to be quick. He watched the alley behind the kid in case he had a shadow, a guard or a watcher to make sure he delivered the goods. No sign of anyone. The kid was alone. Denny stayed perfectly still in the shadow of an alcove in the windowless wall.

The kid walked past him. Denny was sure the kid's eyes flicked in his direction and he thought he saw a smile on the small face, but the kid didn't break stride. It was a boy of about twelve, Denny guessed, and he can't have seen anything or he'd be scared.

Ah, the old days, in the gang with Bob and Pete and Scabby Ted. We used to have so much fun with the little kids. Scabby Ted pissed off somewhere three years ago. Pete turned straight and scared, I wonder what he's doing now?

Denny slid the long thin knife from its sheath, *Just have to get rich all on my own, I suppose.* He moved in silence, came up behind the boy. One hand over the mouth and a quick cut across the throat. The boy made no sound, he simply fell. Denny grabbed the bag, resheathed his knife – no time to clean it now – and ran along the alley.

At the street, he relaxed into a casual stroll, the bag over his shoulder. Just another man in a mask, carrying home a work bag. Just like everyone else. The mask hid his grin. *This is just too damn easy.*

Denny's flat was small, but then there was only him and he didn't need much space. A bigger place would just mean more cleaning. It was a decent flat, rented from the local council and, he always thought, it was pleasant enough.

He placed the bag on the kitchen table. It was really quite heavy and he wondered how that scrawny kid had managed to carry it so easily. His fingers itched to open it but... *Patience. I have all night and I need a drink.*

He poured a large vodka and added a splash of lemonade. His knife lay in the sink, it had moved so fast there was only a trace of blood on it from the kid's throat. The leather sheath had gained an addition to its spreading collection of bloodstains but Denny saw that as a kind of scorecard. The staining darkened over time. Gave the sheath character.

He took a swig of vodka and stared at the bag. It was well used, worn and wrinkled. There was a splash of blood down one side. Denny smiled. Seems nobody had noticed on his way home but then it was Halloween, it was dark, and everyone was too busy having fun.

What could be in there? It felt too heavy for cash. Maybe too heavy for drugs. Stolen jewellery perhaps? Denny took another swig. Maybe the kid was homeless and it was all just worthless shit. He shook his head. That kid was clean and healthy, he hadn't been sleeping rough. Finally setting down his glass, Denny reached for the bag's drawstring and pulled the top open.

"I'm supposed to give you one chance."

Denny started at the voice. He looked around but saw nobody.

"I don't want to. Look in the bag."

The boy stood opposite him, on the other side of the table, between Denny and the sink where his work knife lay.

"How the hell did you get in here?" *How the hell are you alive? And why do you look familiar?*

"It doesn't matter. Soon it will be over, or maybe I should say it will begin." The boy smiled. "Do you remember me?" He lifted his head. Scars criss-crossed his neck, one of them recently healed.

"It can't be. That was seven years ago." Denny ran his tongue over his dry lips. *That kid died, and if he had lived he'd be an adult now.*

"I won't tell you my name. You and your friends never asked for it. After the things you did, I have no reason to give you the one last chance I'm supposed to but those are the rules. So, I'm supposed to tell you not to look in the bag." The boy leaned forward. "I have to tell you what's inside."

Denny swallowed, the vodka buzz in his head making this whole thing feel unreal. "Well? What's inside?"

The boy grinned. "Your darkest dream. Your wildest imaginings. A thing beyond mere money and human materialism. Eternity. A thing whose value can never be counted. Whether you look inside is up to you. I cannot force you either way. It is entirely your decision." The boy sniffed. "If you don't want to look then I take the bag and go. Then you'll never know."

Denny took a breath and regretted it. The alcohol surged in his veins. "If I open it, do I get to keep what's inside?"

"Yes, I suppose that's one way of putting it." The boy smiled at the floor. "If you look inside, the bag becomes yours. If not, I take it and leave."

I should have added less vodka and more lemonade. The alcohol fuzzed Denny's thoughts. He narrowed his eyes. "There's a trick here, isn't there?"

"Yes." The boy answered at once. "I don't want you to know in advance what's in the bag. It is a thing of great value to me. So yes, I am trying to trick you." The boy's smile never wavered. "Even so, the choice is always yours. You can look in the bag or I take it away. Make your choice."

It had been rather a large glass of vodka. Denny struggled to make sense of the conflicting thoughts in his head. The boy could not be here. He could not be who he claimed to be, that boy was dead. If he had somehow survived, he'd be close to twenty now. If it was him he had no reason to reward Denny for the horrors they had inflicted on him. If he was a ghost, how could the bag be real? It was real, solid and heavy. It contained something important and the boy didn't want him to know what it was. That last thought beat out the others. The bag had something of value in it and Denny wanted it.

Denny reached for the bag. He pulled the top open wide and looked inside.

Bob stared up at him

Denny wanted to recoil, to close the bag, to forget the severed head he had seen, with its moving eyes and silent mouthings of horror but he could not look away. He had to watch as the head decayed at a frightening speed until it became a skull, then drop into an abyss of flame. *It's like the bag is a portal to Hell.*

"It is." The boy's voice seemed far away. "You stay in the bag until I get the next one. Then your head goes to Hell."

Denny wanted to answer but the cracking in his neck prevented it. Vertebrae separated, muscles tore, tendons turned to jelly. Then he was looking up, out of the bag, at a headless body that slid out of his line of sight. All he could see was his ceiling.

The boy's face smiled down at him. "You won't be in there too long. I have one more to find. Once that's done, I get to rest." He sniffed. "You see, I didn't completely hate what you did, even though I was terrified and forced into it, so I was condemned to Hell anyway. I despised you and your friends for that more than anything. It turns out my hate was strong enough to do a deal. If I deliver your four souls before you have a chance to redeem yourselves – not that any of you are likely to try – then I get released."

Denny moved his mouth but no sound came out.

"Oh forget it, you have no lungs and no larynx now. You'll never speak again." The boy gathered the drawstrings. "In Hell you will be a silent head and nothing more. Only the demons will hear the music of your screams."

Denny moved his jaw. *What about Pete? He was the one who went back to normal life. This kid can't get him now.*

"The last one is Edward Scabrous. The one you called Scabby Ted." The kid's face disappeared as he pulled on the drawstring. "Your friend Pete was the first I caught. He'd become a scoutmaster. He liked small boys."

Darkness enveloped the interior of the bag. All that was left was the feeling of the bag being lifted and the boy's last words.

"As did you."

Dust Mote Halloween

Wandra Nomad

Kirk and Bob, having been among the first humans transitioned into pure consciousness in a mass about the size of a dust mote, were watching a huge football stadium fade to nothing.

"I just love the way this happens after we've transitioned the thousands of humans who only moments ago packed this place," said Bob.

Motioning toward several dogs that were roaming around the natural area of grass and shrubs that appeared in place of the stadium, Kirk said, "Once they get over the shock of it I imagine they'll find life much simpler now." The dogs were sniffing everything and appearing a bit bewildered.

"Poor things! They're probably searching for their former security guard partners," said Bob. "Seems a bit harsh on them, doesn't it?"

"Not really. When the 'voices' primed the human race to seek transition apparently the 'voices from outer space' also primed 'human dependent' animals to either revert to being more 'natural' or to fade away with the rest of the surroundings," Kirk explained.

"Oh, that's good! At least there won't be a bunch of Fifis or Whiskers roaming around distressed. So, where shall we head next?"

"Let's check the clock tower to see if Carlotta is there," suggested Kirk.

"OK, I'm still not sure how much she can accomplish on her own yet."

"True, but she's still doing better than the first guy they transitioned."

"I thought Carlotta was the first."

"I know, but the guy before her was an even tougher case."

"How?

"Let's go to the clock tower first. I've been suggesting to him and some others that they might want to touch base there now and then."

Adam

"Well that took less than the blink of an eye," said Bob, "not that we *have* eyes! So now Kirk, are you going to tell me ..."

"Hello?" said Kirk. "Who is here besides Bob and me?"

"Me," said both Carlotta and a distinctly different voice.

"Adam?" asked Kirk.

"Yeah, so, who's the others?"

"Carlotta and Bob. I was just telling Bob that Carlotta was not the first person to be transitioned."

What! yelped Carlotta.

"True, Carlotta, and Adam here has quite a story to tell. Adam, why don't you bring them up to date on your experience."

"Well – um – how much of it?"

"Just start at the beginning and tell us as much as you are comfortable sharing." Kirk replied reassuringly.

"Gulp! Well, the beginning – ummm – well I was born rather tiny and never got very big. I was picked on and ridiculed all my life so I just retreated and was rather shy – umm – not at all adventurous. From when I was very young I became cautious, fearful even and learned to keep out of the path of other people. But, to get more current, I started getting bugged by ghosts. Nothing I could see but I heard them talking about me."

Ah-ha! The voices! said Carlotta. *And they wanted you to change?*

"Well not really – umm – not me really. There I was sitting in deep shadows on my porch in the dark because it was Halloween. And even though my house is – umm was – well, still is – pretty secluded, I never put on a light at Halloween. So I was sitting there alone in the dark."

Get on with it! thought Carlotta.

"Then these ghosts were talking to me. They called me the 'first human' and said all would follow forth from me. I had no idea what was going on."

"First human?" asked Bob. "Like the in "Adam and Eve" Adam?"

"I guess maybe – anyway they changed me. Kirk has another word for that."

"Transitioned," said Kirk

"Yeah that."

"Why'd you agree?" asked Bob. "You said you are not adventuresome."

"Well – I had no choice – did I? They just did it."

Without asking you to imagine – ummm –...

"No! Not anything! Kirk told me how it was for you but not for me. One minute I was me and the next I was – umm – whatever it is that I am now."

"Wow!" Bob and Carlotta exclaimed together.

"Yeah! When I realized I was no longer in my body I sort of panicked and searched around for it.

"I screamed 'Where's my body?' but all I heard was sort of a whisper, 'No longer needed.'"

"I disagreed and careened all over the porch and then in the house and even went back out and searched the yard. But I – umm – my body – had just disappeared."

You didn't have to figure out how to move around? asked Carlotta.

"Umm – No. I was just too frantic to find my body! I was looking anywhere and everywhere. I wandered pretty far checking every bump and shadow I could see in the dark."

Amazing! And no one helped you learn how?

"No and I never gave a thought to how I could do that. I started seeing the kids out trick or treating in all their various costumes. Kids usually tease or threaten me. I didn't stop to think that they couldn't see me and shouted at them. Some of them seemed startled and a few seemed pretty scared.

"It may not be very nice of me but I've been tormented most of my life so I was pretty pleased that I'd scared them and shouted even more. Most of their costumes were pretty unconvincing so I'm afraid I even sneered at a few of them." Adam paused.

"Well I was actually having a pretty good time until I noticed that one of the witches looked more authentic. It was actually zigzagging around up in the air. And cackling! I'd imagined witches cackling but to hear it was shocking! I gasped and it noticed but seemed unable to see me." He paused.

"Can *you* see me? Or see each other?" he asked.

Adam and the others all said, "No."

Then Kirk added, "But sometimes in a beam of sunlight I seem to see a fleck or a tiny sparkle but I've never been sure if it was just a dust mote or one of us. But, you were saying ...?"

"Right. Well I asked that witch if she was real and she asked 'why not? this *is The Night of Witches*.' I remembered reading somewhere about that being one of the things Halloween is called — somewhere."

"Really?" asked Bob? "So it was a real witch?"

"Well, I didn't hang around to find out. The very idea spooked me so I zipped away from there as fast as I could!"

Figures! said Carlotta rather sarcastically.

Ignoring her, Adam continued. "As I calmed down I began to notice the air was filling with things I never thought were real. Like huge spiders weaving enormous webs and gigantic bats emitting high pitched squeaks – some even attacking the humongous spiders. I got terrified and careened away!"

Carlotta made another disgusted snort.

"Still hanging on to a bit of skepticism I tried to reason with myself saying it was over active imagination triggered by fear. I calmed myself down a bit. But gradually I was aware that I was not alone.

"What at first appeared as wisps of fog or mist seemed to take on shapes and float about less aimlessly. Some seemed focused on the spot where I was hovering."

"Ghosts?" asked Bob?

"I began to think so, and tried to drift away but one of them seemed to notice me."

It asked, "What are you?"

"Can you see me?"

"Not really but I know you are there."

"At that, several of the other figures – ummm ghosts – drifted toward us."

"Yes!" some exclaimed. "What are you?"

"How tasty might it be?" asked one.

"That made me remember that another name for Halloween is *The Hungry Ghost Festival*! I fled again, but I soon convinced myself I was just letting my imagination run too wild."

"I passed a kid in a devil's costume and remembered Halloween can also be called *The Devil's Holiday*. But this was so obviously a kid in costume I had to laugh at myself." Adam laughed.

"To help me calm down I looked for a quiet place to relax. Besides my own porch I've always been fond of cemeteries."

You? Carlotta scoffed!

"Yeah, me! They are places most people avoid, except during funerals, and especially after dark. I thought about a large cemetery I'd often visited to walk and think. Instantly I was there and began to feel calmer."

"Along the walls and gates kids were loudly decorating it in toilet tissue but in the interior I found the solace I was seeking.

"Assessing my situation I began to realize my body and I might not get reunited. Thinking back I remembered hearing 'No longer needed' but that was it."

They didn't tell you that you'd 'figure it out'? Carlotta asked.

"Nope – nothing."

And I thought I got shafted!

"I think they had great hopes for you and tried to help you more."

Why do you think that?

"I'm coming to that."

So get on with it! thought the ever impatient Carlotta.

"While calming down in my favorite cemetery, I tried to figure out what had happened to me. I considered but soon rejected the idea that I was dreaming it all. I looked around for supporting evidence figuring there wouldn't be any in the cemetery.

"To my astonishment I was not alone. On or near several of the graves were silent people. Why would they be here? There was no one to 'trick or treat'. And no signs of a party going on. I mused that Halloween was just the time one might expect a party in a cemetery but nothing indicated this was a party. And though some seemed dressed in costumes suitable to a cemetery or even an accident scene – there was no merry making.

"Who are you? Why are you here?" I asked.

A few turned toward me.

"Well why not?" one asked.

I sighed. "Oh don't give me that '*Night of Witches*' crap" I said. "That's been tried and I've already rejected it."

"Well, maybe you have," answered one of them, "but it *is* their night. And it is also ours, which is much more significant for us don't you think? But I'm wondering why I still bother."

Bits of uneasiness began poising themselves ready to dart through my mind.

"What do you mean?" I asked.

"Well everyone who had meaning for me have already joined us – so why bother?"

"What do you mean?" I asked again.

"Well human life is short but death is for eternity."

"So?" Those bits of uneasiness were becoming sharper.

"Well as you can see I wasn't young when I got here, and after being here for a few hundred years or more – there's no one familiar here for me to see. And if I try I am ignored or trigger terror. I guess I just come to observe the changes in the way of life."

"What do y-you mean?" I knew I was starting to sound like a broken record, but keeping those icicles at bay was becoming so difficult it was getting hard to form words. I did notice that while some of the others were nodding in agreement others were heading toward the gates.

"You don't know? This is the *Day of the Dead* or Halloween more commonly around here. But why they call it 'day' when we can only come out in full darkness baffles me."

"Yeah, I heard that but ..."

"Then I saw him – the lone figure dressed in black and carrying a scythe. As he marched up to us most of the others backed away. Behind him were a few reluctant looking followers. *The Grim Reaper*! He pointed a finger at me and in a voice that made my icicles grow icicles he said, 'Do not mess with what is mine!'

"Wham! The icicles won. I found myself cowering on my porch. And there I stayed until Kirk came along."

That's it?

"Well no. While I was there on the porch I heard voices – your 'Voices' I think, Carlotta."

Well are you ever planning to tell us? Carlotta demanded sarcastically.

"Carlotta, ease up a bit, will yah?" said Kirk. "Continue, Adam."

"I have no idea how long I was there – I find that time seems to have little meaning now."

The others made sounds of agreement.

"Eventually I felt calmer and began noticing sounds, well, actually voices, around me. They seemed to find me a failure – according to them, I hadn't even begun my task. That I had no idea what task they meant seemed never to have occurred to them, I had no desire to find out so I maintained my silence.

"They seemed to be in disagreement on how to move forward with their own mission. Some believed that my physical mass though considerable by their standards had been insufficient; others thought they should be focusing on humans with more imaginative minds. Finally they seemed to have found one to fit both criteria and left me alone."

"That was Carlotta!" said Bob

"I believe so," said Adam.

"After the Halloween they'd given me I've been happy to be rid of them. They never did enlighten me as to what my task was supposed to have been. By the time they left me I'd grown accustomed to having no body. I could even see some advantages and was happy to be ignored. Well, until Kirk showed up and clarified things for me."

"So now you are one of us?" Bob asked. "And our mission?"

"Well I guess – but it's all very new to me."

Happy Halloween muttered Carlotta in disgust!

What Time Do You Finish?

Roo B. Doo

It is said that Halloween is the time of year when the veil between dimensions is worn at its thinnest. In the year 2020, when a global viral pandemic, violent rioting and supermarket socially distanced queues dominated everyday life, that boundary thickness could be considered as flimsy as paper medical face mask. Why, an errant finger could easily pierce it.

Shit!

God adjusted the mask across her visage, hoping no one would notice the ragged hole, and that nothing too nasty had fallen through the breach on her sweet breath.

"How the hell am I supposed to know when we are?" Death snapped and glared up from inside the impenetrable blackness of his cowl at the three ominous figures surrounding him. They stood huddled at the junction of Great Russell and Bloomsbury Streets in London's bustling West End. It was night, it was cold and, save for the motley quartet, the streets were completely deserted.

"Becoz yur Death," the first figure hissed and bared vampiric fangs. Famine appeared tall and angular, dressed in a tuxedo, silk lined cape, and a countenance so pale, it could only have been achieved by avoiding sunlight at any and all costs.

"Because you have the contraption," the second figure added angrily. War appeared to be a smart businesswoman, confident and aggressive, in horn-rimmed glasses, sharp suit and infinitely sharper stiletto heels.

"AAAAAAAGH!" the third figure groaned as a fat, black fly zig-zagged across a sunken cheek, before disappearing into a filth-caked nostril. Pestilence appeared to be a zombie; slack mouthed, grey decaying flesh and milk white, opaque eyes.

"No, Pesto, I don't know what happened to the horses." Death answered his rotting companion. He pulled himself up to his full height of three feet and three inches and retrieved a battered Psion organiser from beneath the folds of his robe. He unsheathed it with a satisfying *pop*. "I don't understand it," he cried, "transport's always been laid on before."

War, Famine and Pestilence stood in silence, watching over the diminutive but perfectly formed grim reaper, as he punched the keys of the electronic organiser with a gleaming phalange, and waited.

Click. Click. Click, click, click... click.

"Well?" War said impatiently. "We're in London, that much is for sure. The British Museum is over there."

Pestilence's body did not move a single rotting muscle, but his head turned an unearthly 180° to follow the direction that War's crimson painted talon was pointing in. "UGH WAAAGH AAAAAAAGH!"

"Ve don't know if ve are zupposed to go zere." Famine reached out and clasped either side of Pestilence's head, twisting it back into a front facing position. "Ve don't know vy ve are even here. Death, vot iz taking you zo long to find out?"

"Wait..." Death did not look up.

Click. Click, click. Click.

Death peered hard at the tiny screen on the Psion, before shaking it hard. "I dunno. It's not working. Maybe the Cosmic Consciousness Neural Net is down again," he said with a shrug.

"Argh!" War howled. She reached down and grabbed Death by the front of his robe and lifted him up to face height. Behind her glasses, War's eyes blazed with fire. "That's just brilliant! Ace! Fun-fucking-tastic, Death! What are we meant to do now?"

The dead weight of Pestilence's arm slapped War on the shoulder. "WAAAGH UGH!"

"Yez, yez, yez, ve should all calm down," Famine said smoothly, pulling Death from War's tight grasp and setting him back on the pavement. He plucked Pestilence's arm from War's shoulder before she could rip it from its socket. "It does no good for uz to get agitated. Ve need to zink vot haz happened."

"Exactly right, Famine. Let's look at what we do know." Death pushed himself free of the huddle and turned to face his companions. "We've got War, Famine, Pestilence and yours truly." He began to glide, circling his companions. "The ultimate harbingers of doom and bringers of great tribulation. The Four Horsemen of the Apocalypse-"

"AAAAAAAGH UGH!"

"*Sans* horses, indeed. Most irregular. Literally dropped, without warning, in the middle of London-"

"Clos to ze British Muzeum," Famine interrupted.

"Correct. So we know *where* we are but we don't know *when* we are-"

"Late twentieth, early twenty first century, I'd say, from the smell of the air," War joined in. "Plus it's night time and it's bloody freezing."

"A winter's night, yes. Probably accounts for the lack of any activity about-"

"UGH!"

Death glided to a stop. "Your right, Pesto; there should be people about, even in winter, big city like this produces lots of traffic-"

Famine tapped on his fangs in contemplation. "Yez, no motor vehicles hav passed by since ve arrived."

Death nodded slowly, then looked up at the sky. One by one, War, Famine and Pestilence followed Death's gaze.

"Nope, too much cloud cover and light pollution. I can't see any stars to work out when we are."

"I have a very bad feeling about this," War whispered hoarsely.

"WAAAGH AAAAAAAGH!" Pestilence groaned.

"I agree, Pestilence, my dear friend. It haz to be a mistake," Famine said solemnly. "An accident."

"Possibly. We'd better start walking," Death said and glided away down Bloomsbury Street, in the direction of Covent Garden.

War, Famine and Pestilence looked at each other and muttered darkly.

"Hold it, short-arse," War barked. "Where exactly are we walking to? I can't go far in these heels. They're fucking murder."

Pestilence dropped a shoulder and lurched awkwardly after Death. "AAAAAAAGH WAAAGH AAAAAAAGH!"

"Seriously? You're going to follow him?" War shouted after the hunched and shambling figure of Pestilence. "You'll disintegrate before you reach the end of this street, you noxious pile of pus!"

Famine took War's hands between his own, bowed deeply and kissed her clenched fists open. "Don't vorry, my dear lady. I vill speak to Death." Gently, he tugged on War so that she tottered forward with unsteady steps. "Please, come, valk slowly. I vill talk to him." With that, Famine turned into a giant bat and flew off in the direction of Death.

War roared with frustration but continued to follow the others. "I have Birkenstocks, you know. Why couldn't I have manifested in my fucking Birkenstocks..."

Death heard wop-wopping wing beats approach from behind, and felt the change in air pressure as Famine flew over his head. He glided slowly until he reached his suave compadre, who stood in the middle of the pavement, arms wide, cape billowing and fangs bared.

"Death, stop please," Famine pleaded. "Vor and Pestilence are in no fit state to valk far. Look." He gestured back to the way they'd come. Pestilence jerked along slowly in the middle distance, with War following on behind, daintily sidestepping the trail of fleshy ooze left in Pestilence's wake.

"Death, Death," Famine cooed, "You know ve vould valk to the ends of ze vorld vid you, but you must tell us, vere are you taking us?"

Death paused and looked up, appraising his companion – Famine: always hungry, never sated, forever empty; his vampire appearance was more than apt. Pestilence, too, in zombie form was unrelenting, poisoning everything, even the very air. War, however, was a puzzler unless she represented a battle of the sexes. Should War shatter the fabled glass ceiling, Death was certain she would then set about slitting every available throat with the deadly shards.

What about me, though? I'm exactly the same, I haven't changed, Death wondered. The inside of his skull began to itch. He sighed and shook his head. This whole situation was wrong and he couldn't shake the feeling that he was missing something. Something big. Something important.

"Death?" Famine snapped his fingers rapidly. "Vere are ve going?" he demanded.

"To the Embankment, Famine. To Cleopatra's Needle."

"Ov course!" Famine slap the palm of his hand against his widow's peaked forehead. "Ze ancient Egyptian Obelisks of Time! Ve can return to ze hintervorld by way ov Cleopatra's Needle! Zat iz super fine zinking, Death. No vonder yur the leader."

"I-" Death suddenly cocked his head to one side. "Can you hear that?"

There was a low rumble in the distance but it was gradually getting louder, moving nearer. Death and Famine watched as at first, War turned her head to look behind, following the direction of the sound, then Pestilence slowly shuffled round to see what was making the noise. Further back in the distance, Death could just make out a dim rectangle of orange light, floating closer through the darkness, getting brighter. War began to wave her arms and shout.

"AAAAAAAGH!" Pestilence bellowed.

Death and Famine glanced at each other before racing back towards Pestilence and War. "**Taxi!**" they shouted in unison, tinged of relief.

War, Famine and Pestilence sat in abject silence in the back of the taxi, separated from Death and the taxi driver in the front by a transparent sheet of plexiglass, with only a narrow slot cut into it for the exchange of money.

Excuse me while I light my spliff...

"Spliff," the taxi driver sang along to the bassy sound of Bob Marley and the Wailers coming through the speakers.

Oh God I gotta take a lift...

"Lift." The taxi driver turned toward Death and gave him a beaming smile.

From reality I just can't drift...

"Drift."

That's why I am staying with this riff...

"Riff." The taxi driver chuckled and tapped his hands on the top of the steering wheel, in time with the music. "Easy skanking. Hell, I love this song."

Death looked out of his side window. The feeling that something was wrong had only intensified as the empty London streets rushed by. He cursed the broken Psion organiser tucked inside his robes. *Bloody useless technology. Give me an hourglass any day*, he thought sourly.

"Was it a good party?" the taxi driver asked.

"Huh?" Death replied, perplexed by the driver's question.

The taxi driver laughed. "The fancy dress party. Your costumes are sweet. I thought the government had cancelled Halloween because of the Rona."

Death stiffened and the itching inside his skull increased. "Halloween's been cancelled?"

"Yeah man, Christmas too if we're not lucky," the taxi driver replied.

"What year is it?" Death asked slowly.

The taxi driver sucked his teeth contemptuously. "What you mean *what year is it?* It's 2020, child. Where have you been?"

A burst of realisation exploded through Death's train of consciousness: *It's 2020: the year anything happened!* The year when pandemic waves of Coronavirus and Karenitus swept the globe, resulting in lockdowns, economic disaster and civil unrest. *Things are starting to make sense now!* Even so, the itch continued to irritate the inside of Death's skull.

Cigar smoke suddenly filled the front of the taxi. Death coughed and tapped on the sign affixed to the console. "That says 'No Smoking'."

The taxi driver grinned at Death, a smoking cigar butt jauntily perched from the corner of his mouth. "2020, child. Donch ya know the saying? 'A smoke a day keeps the Rona at bay'." He laughed heartily and bounced up and down in his seat with mirth. "Besides, who's gonna stop me? Look about you, my small friend. There's no one around to say shit about it."

If Death still had eyes, they would have been rolling round his ocular cavities. "Hey guys." He shouted to the others through the slot in the plexiglass. "Problem solved: it's 2020."

"Tventy Tventy! Hellz Bellz!" Famine exclaimed.

Pestilence gave a guttural groan. "WAAAGH UGH AAAAAAAGH!"

"Yes, but what's the date?" War demanded nervously.

"It's the 31st October, sugar," the taxi driver called back. "Happy Halloween."

The taxi stopped at the end of Temple Place. In front lay the deserted Embankment. Along side it, the river Thames flowed swiftly past, glittering lights shimmered on its rippled surface, as above the clouds began to clear. The taxi driver nonchalantly flicked a switch on his dashboard, locking all the vehicle doors with a loud *clunk*.

"Oh no," War murmured gravely and pressed her hands hard against her stomach. "No, no, no!"

"Vot iz it, Vor?" Famine asked with rising alarm.

A shaft of moonlight hit the taxi as it slowly pulled out right onto the Embankment and illuminated its interior. The Moon was bright, it was clear and it was very full.

"It's my monthlies," War whined, sliding off her seat and onto all fours. Her jaw elongated and wiry tufts of fur sprang from her gnarly brow, knocking War's horn-rimmed glasses from her face. "I don't fucking believe this. Why nowOOOO!"

"Now *this* is a great song. One of the Skipper's best," the taxi driver exclaimed, ignoring the howling and growling and shrieks of panic coming from the back, as smart and professional War transformed into a ferocious and carnal beast. He turned up the volume on his stereo and began to croon along, "*Until the philosophy, which hold one race superior and another. Inferior. Is finally. And permanently. Discredited. And abandoned. Everywhere is war. Me say war.*"

"Vot? NOOOO! Get avay! Get avay!" Famine screamed and impotently fumbled with the taxi's doors handles. They were securely locked, however; there would be no escape.

Death sat stock still, strapped in tight and listened in horror to the sound of Famine and Pestilence being ripped apart by the slavering jaws and slashing claws of a werewolf that appeared to be War.

"How's you seat, child?" the taxi driver slyly asked.

"I'm not a child," Death replied tersely.

"UGH!" Pestilence's bloody fingers abruptly thrust through the slot in the plexiglass, twitched once, then lay limp.

"I know, I know, little man. No offence intended." The taxi driver continued. "That space you're occupying used to be for luggage, but times are hard and last year it was converted into a child seat," he explained. "Good thing for you, eh?"

The heavy silence that fell between the driver and his passenger was punctured by the sound of wet chomps and crunching bone from behind.

The itch in Death skull stopped, but the very fabric of reality now took up its cause.

"Scratch?" Death asked tentatively.

"Yes, child."

"*Old* Scratch?"

"Who else you expecting?" the Devil, who appeared to be a smirking, smoking taxi driver, replied. The vehicle slowed to a stop next to Cleopatra's Needle. "Now hurry up and spit it out. It's time for you to leave."

Death paused; it felt like eternity. Finally he asked, "Why?"

"*Why?*" Old Scratch puffed on his cigar, the shit-eating grin never leaving his face. "Why, Armageddon, little man. What did you think this is?"

Death was flummoxed. In his long existence, he had never been flummoxed before. It was a new sensation, but not one he'd ever longed for.

Old Scratch patted him on the head, then reached up to retrieve a folded piece of paper from behind the sun visor. "I got a letter last year, see," he explained. He unfolded the page and glanced down at the childish writing on it. "From a sweet, innocent child. A touch dyslexic, but with the purest soul ever to inhabit a human body. What could I do?" He offer the letter to Death. "My heart just melted."

Death took the letter from Old Scratch and began to read aloud: "*Dear Satan. My name is Molly and I have everything I will ever need. Can you please help everybody else in the world by ending hunger, pollution and war. This is my Christmas wish. Thank you. Molly Darling, age 6. P.S. I hope you are well.*"

All the stars in the heavens swirled furiously inside Death's skull. He mentally grappled with the raging storm, searching for a handhold on his sanity. "War ended Pestilence and Famine, but War isn't dead."

"You sure? Can't hear no breathing back there."

Death swiftly unlocked his seatbelt and stood up on his seat. The plexiglass was no longer transparent, but smeared red with blood and gore. He pushed the dead fingers of Pestilence back through the slot and heard a splash as the severed hand they were attached to thudded to the floor of the taxi. Death peered through the gap and saw War lying naked and smooth in the bloodbath. A chunk of half chewed greenish meat fell free from her lifeless lips.

"WooEE! That Pesto sure was ripe!" Old Scratch said, opening his window and flicking out ash from his cigar. "Bad meat. Never eat it. Always, *always*, insist on fresh."

Death pulled away from the sight of the abomination in the back of the taxi and sat back down in his seat. "But how can it be Armageddon if War, Famine and Pestilence are gone?"

Old Scratch punched the numbers on the keyboard of the fare display on the dashboard. "With no hunger, there will be obesity, so humanity will become slovenly and fat, lazy and satisfied. No war means no competition, no goals to achieve, so mankind will lose its desire to better itself. And the elimination of pollution is a sure fire way of killing any human creativity. I give the species ten years, tops."

"But there will be death," Death whispered softly.

"Oh indeed, you're still needed. You have a busy time ahead of you, little man. That'll be six six six."

Death snapped his head back to face the Devil in the driver's seat. "What?"

Old Scratch laughed and pointed to the fare metre. He gave a phlegmy cough and waved Death away. "Just kidding. For you, child, no charge," he said gleefully.

Horseman of the Year Award

Mark Ellott

Halloween, 2020 – the Green Room.

It was that time of the year. As the seasons of the sun turned towards winter and the nights grew long and cold, the demons and ghouls, the denizens of the other world, would rise up for one night together. And on that one night they would hold their awards ceremony as it was a suitable time to reflect on the achievements of the year. The Horseman of the Year award was given to the one rider who was deemed to have caused the most Earthly chaos during the year.

Halloween was always a bit of a joke for the awards as far as Death was concerned as he had been out of the running for so many years now that he had all but given up hope of another win, but maybe this would be his year. Eventually. For such a dour personality, the concept of hope lurking in his soul would seem to many a contradiction, but lurk it did nonetheless.

Indeed, some uncharitable types had referred to him mentioning his last winning of the award in 1351 as being much like an England football fan going on and on and on about 1966 as if something momentous had occurred that year. It was embarrassing, War told him on one occasion when he asked if she could recall the event when he last won. "*But,*" Death retorted, "*You have had far too many opportunities.*"

1666 looked as if it was in the bag at one point, but Pestilence swiped it from under his nose, much to his chagrin. Death did wonder to himself if Pestilence had something on the judges, but could find no evidence, so he sighed to himself and remained morose about the whole thing, like some ethereal Eeyore.

Death was present in the green room awaiting the call—present, but not entirely with the group, setting himself apart almost as a disinterested observer as the time rolled on towards midnight.

War leaned back and sipped her whisky, watching as the amber liquid swirled around her glass, catching the light and tempting her with its smoothness. There was something malevolent and beautiful about her smile as she looked across at Death, he noted. On the surface she may have been relaxed but there was a tension in her body, like a rattler ready to strike. Deadly fast and merciless. Death scowled. No wonder she was pleased with herself, she had picked up multiple awards during the 100 years' war, and then again twice in the twentieth century and that bastard Blair had given her another opportunity in the early twenty first. He glanced down idly at his smartphone and shook his head sadly. Still no notification for that bugger. *There's no justice in the world.* The Devil really did look after his own, he thought.

But that was the problem, Death told himself – war brought death to millions as did Pestilence and Famine, but he didn't get the glory, they did and it wasn't fair. They would come sweeping in causing their chaos and he was left to do the cleaning up, like the char lady who did a fine job, but no one asked her name. None of them could do their jobs without him, but they kept getting Horseman of the Year like some little macabre cartel and he was repeatedly left out. Surely it was his turn this time. He cast a sulky glance at the others as they sat lounging in the easy chairs sipping their drinks and waiting for the call.

Halloween at midnight when the announcement ceremony took place was a time for humiliation for Death and he wondered why he put up with it. Maybe, he told himself, he should just boycott the whole thing. Leave them to it with their mutual backslapping and planet-sized egos. Go for a long ride. Find some excuse to be elsewhere for the night. There was a Ducati sports bike just waiting for his attention.

He thought about this for a while, then his attention flipped to War and her successes. Perhaps he should groom a politician, after all, there were plenty to choose from. That Chinese chap seemed to him to be an amenable cove. Anyway, this year was looking good. Not as hopeful as it seemed in January, but that little bug getting out of China had indeed put everyone on panic and he had been pretty busy in that part of the world at the turn of the year, before rushing off to Europe and cleaning up in Italy then off to Spain, back to Italy and eventually the UK. And where was Pestilence then, eh? In the pub, where he usually was. But it was Death who rode along afterwards doing all the heavy lifting. None of these three would be any use without him, the unsung hero of the quartet. He snorted to himself at the thought.

He had considered Putin, but much to his annoyance, War had got there before him. Although, he reflected, the man's influence wasn't what it was cracked up to be—a few squabbles in Chechnya and the Crimea that fizzled out to nothing very much. A paper tiger really, all brawn and no brain, Death figured. War could keep him. Macron had looked promising for a while, but Death recoiled at the thought. Too second rate for his liking. Weak, insipid and incompetent. Who would want him for a lieutenant? It would reflect badly on his recruitment skills, he decided.

He took a sip of the whisky. At least these award events provided decent beverages, he mused. This one was a single malt and ran down the throat in a warm glow. Well, it would if he had a throat, but he made the most of it.

He looked around the room at his companions. War, the only woman in the group, was a lithe brunette in tight black leather jacket and jeans with dark eyes and tattoos on her neck. Had she had a new one since he last saw her?

"This one?" she asked, in response to his query. She pointed to the snake that ran down her neck to her partially exposed breast and disappeared somewhere in her ample cleavage, upon which Death's gaze lingered just a little too long. "Yeah, this is new. Rather good, isn't it? I'll give you the name of my tattooist if you like."

Death lifted a bony hand to the light.

"Ah," she said. "Of course. Just a thought."

"I like it," Pestilence said. Death looked across at his associate. Thin leathery skin fell in folds about the skinny body and flies buzzed around him, but he always seemed unperturbed by these tiny travelling companions. Death might have been irritated by such accompaniment, but they left the others alone, preferring to remain close to Pestilence, who, from time to time would swat one of them and place it on his reptilian tongue and swallow it. He did so now, whereupon he ran his tongue across his lips and smiled as the dead fly was immediately replaced with another from nowhere.

"Think you will get it this year?" he asked Death. "After all, the wars haven't been up to much. Just over half a million dead from the virus. Although, to be fair, it was my virus." He smiled again with a pleased expression.

"Not much of a virus if you ask me," Famine said easily. The others looked at him as he pulled his cape closer around his gaunt body. "Well come on... I'm sure you could have come up with something more effective. Half a million deaths out of sixty-two billion? You weren't even trying. You did a better job with swine flu."

"Well..." Pestilence retorted irritably, his body stiffening with indignation, "I didn't see much effort from you this year. Africa is what it has always been. No new global warming Saharan desert across Europe wiping out half the population, despite your promises year after year. I'm beginning to think you don't have it in you anymore. You're all talk and no trousers."

Death thought that Pestilence had a point. These days, the best that Famine could do was the usual African gig. Nothing changed. Famine did have a small panic attack back in 1985 and that cost him the award that year, leaving him a runner up. Although Sir Bob hadn't made a dent in Famine's long term survival, it occurred to Death that it had damaged his confidence. It was small stuff these days. Not since biblical times and the glory days of plagues of locusts had Famine had a real success. *Just a jobbing horseman,* Death thought. Despite having bought off the IPCC as a job lot, Famine still hadn't quite managed to pull off the big one. Although that new Nile dam might prove promising, if War didn't poke her nose into it first.

On that subject, Death wondered if Trump could be persuaded to get on board. *I'm sure he could help in some small way... Better be quick, though. If he wins this year there's only four years left. And if he doesn't...* He did briefly consider the opposition but quickly dismissed it as they were managing to collapse into undignified defeat quite well on their own without any assistance from their presidential candidate. The likelihood of Biden with his finger on the big red button was so remote, Death thought about putting a few bob on it just in case. But if he did win, the possibilities...

In that moment, Death pondered on humanity's ability to consistently screw things up without divine intervention. He silently raised a glass in admiration for the collective chaos that humanity managed to spread around the globe while he and his colleagues took all the credit.

He started out of his reverie as the others were all squabbling. Well, Pestilence and Famine were exchanging blows while War looked on with an amused smile on her face.

"Stop it," he chided.

She pulled a face and waved her hand and the other two looked a little embarrassed and apologised before sitting back and reaching for a drink.

"Why do you have to keep doing that?" Death asked.

She shrugged. "Because I can," she said. "It's what I do. Check the job description."

"Hmm," Death said. *"So how is that US civil war going?"*

Famine sniggered and War shot him a look, baring her pointed teeth and hissed him into silence. She turned back to Death. "It's a work in progress."

Death raised one of his non-existent eyebrows. *"Really?"*

Pestilence laughed. "Yeah, right, a few protestors take over their cities and do a bit of looting and burning. The Seattle mob even seceded for a while but what a pathetic bunch they turned out to be, all they could manage was to kill their own. Prober job, that."

"I understand that the mob went out into the suburbs, which looked promising," Death said, *"but when the NRA types showed up all armed with automatic rifles, they ran away. Not exactly 1861, is it? As a work in progress, might I humbly suggest that it is in need of considerable effort yet."*

Pestilence laughed and Death caught a waft of his cologne.

"What is that?" he asked.

"Eau de purification," Pestilence said. "I rather like it."

Death refrained from comment and glanced across at War who was scowling at the rest of them with her arms folded and a sneer on her lips.

At least, Death thought, *that has shut her up for a bit.*

They lapsed into silence for a while, sipping their drinks and each absorbed with their own thoughts. Death took the opportunity to light a cigarette. He leaned back and watched the smoke as it drifted up to the ceiling.

"Whose bright idea was it to send Chinese seeds across the world?" Death asked eventually. He had been wondering about that one. A small stroke of genius had it worked.

Famine coughed self-consciously. "That was one of mine. I figured that invasive species spread all over the place would kill off the crops and lead to a famine. Shame I got rumbled, really."

Death shrugged. *"Well, nice try, anyway. I thought it had a touch of class about it."*

Again the room lapsed into an awkward silence. *"Changing the subject,"* Death said, stubbing out the cigarette, *"who is presenting this year?"*

"Vlad," War said.

Death groaned. *"Oh, no, please! Not more werewolf jokes!"*

She grinned, "No. He's on notice. If he tells any werewolf jokes he will be sent on a subconscious bias course."

"Subconscious, my arse!" Famine snorted.

Death inclined his head. *"Well, perhaps those things do have a benefit after all."*

There was a buzz and a light shone in the corner of the room.

War stood up in a fluid move that seemed instantaneous to the observer. "We're on," she said.

The others all stood and followed her out into the auditorium, which by this time, had filled to standing room only. The awards were a popular occasion for the denizens of the darkness and they made the most of the free drinks and nibbles. Death pulled his smartphone out of the folds in his cape and glanced at the screen, longing for the old days when he had a wooden hourglass with a fine brass engraved plate. *Five to midnight.*

He followed the others to an empty table at the foot of the raised stage. At the lectern Vlad was regaling the audience with his jokes and the room erupted into laughter, although Death didn't laugh. He often wondered what it was that people found funny in Vlad's jokes. They usually involved gruesome methods of killing werewolves and having heard one, he felt that he had heard the lot.

As they walked towards the table, the assembly stood and applauded. War raised a fist in salute while Pestilence and Famine acknowledged the tribute with raised hands. Death alone chose to walk as if nothing was happening. *I have my dignity at least,* he thought, watching his companions as they lapped up the adulation.

They took their seats and Vlad once again captured the room, waving a golden envelope in the air.

"Now, ladies and gentlemen and those that aren't sure either way, the moment you have been waiting for…" He paused for effect. "The announcement of this year's Horseman of the Year Award."

"Or woman," War said.

"Well, yes, or woman," Vlad cast her a glance, irritated by the interruption. "Now where was I? Oh, yes, well, there has been plenty that these four have been about this year, I think we can all agree that they have been working hard on our behalf spreading disease, war, famine and death across the globe."

A murmur of assent rippled among the assembled throng.

"Covid-19 at the beginning of the year, riots in cities across most of the West, the imminent collapse of the EU with its ongoing squabbling that might yet lead to more," he winked at War who grinned broadly at the prospect.

"The Chinese seeds…"

Famine half stood and nodded at the crowd. "One of mine."

Vlad shot him a glare and he sat back in his chair. "Some wonderful scams that came out of this, not to mention the confusion, chaos and economic damage. All in all, an excellent job by all involved."

Death couldn't argue with the sentiment but remained silent, awaiting the opening of the envelope. *Perhaps this year, eh?* Perhaps this year they would finally recognise his contribution.

"With no further ado…" Vlad was continuing as Death receded into his inner thoughts. He hated these events. *All inflated egos and no substance,* he acknowledged silently *so why do I bother? Even if I win, I'll hate it.* Perhaps next year he would make his excuses after all.

"Aaaand, the Horseman of the year is…" Vlad opened the envelope and paused for effect, electrifying the room. "The Horsemen of the Year award goes to Pestilence for Covid-19!"

There was a roar as the room erupted into applause and Pestilence stood and walked to the stage, taking his time to absorb the moment and the adulation. Death sank his head in his arms.

Oh, God! He'll be unbearable now!

Pestilence reached the stage and stood next to Vlad, looking pleased with himself, which he was.

"Well," Vlad said as the applause settled down. "That was a well-deserved win, I must say. You wrought worldwide havoc with a nasty flu virus, which was commendable enough, but the panic, alarm and lockdowns was epic, given that it wasn't exactly the Black Death after all."

Everyone looked at Death and a laugh shimmered across the room.

Vlad continued once the laughter died down. "The subsequent economic catastrophe made this one special and all with a relatively low kill rate that set it apart as a work of genius. In England we had some wonderful confusion—masks or no masks and masks in ten days' time, that was a corker. Schools or pubs? Gyms or fast food? Come on, admit it, Boris is one of yours, isn't he?"

Pestilence stiffened. "I couldn't possibly say," he replied haughtily, but everyone knew that denial was confirmation and laughter rippled through the crowd once more—after all, Pestilence had all but denied it and so it must be true.

"Well," Vlad said, "here is the prize. A worthy win." He handed over the much desired golden figurine of a horseman. To rapturous applause Pestilence lifted it above his head in triumph, visibly enjoying the moment.

Eventually the applause settled down and Pestilence looked slightly disappointed that it had died so soon. Awkwardly, he leaned forward to the microphone to make a speech.

Vlad snatched it away. "Just take the award and get off the stage," he hissed. "No one wants a long political speech. Go on, hoppit!"

Pestilence frowned, but complied, holding the figurine over his head as he walked back to the table and sat next to Death.

"Oh well, old bean, commiserations and all that. There's always next year, eh?"

Anonymous

Mark Ellott

My thanks to my sister Sharon for the idea that triggered this story.

Nearly the only light in the dim room was the computer screen. The curtains were pulled closed and only a tiny crack of light trickled into the interior, casting its beam on tired furniture and the faded rug that was in dire need of a visit from Mr. Vacuum Cleaner. On the sofa the remains of last night's pizza were strewn as they congealed in the open boxes, filling the air with the pungent odour of cheese and tomato. On the small coffee table among the stained rings several empty beer cans stood bereft of their contents.

The young man sitting at the keyboard wore his hoodie up so that his pasty face was mostly in shadow. Although not necessary, he felt that it fitted the image. *I am anonymous we are everywhere no system is safe from us, we are the collective.*

Before him, hieroglyphs flashed across the screen, reflecting in his dark eyes. To most people these lines of code would have been a mystery, but to the hacker, they were a roadmap. A roadmap to a computer system and one that he could follow much as the rest of us would follow the signs on the Great North Road saying "North". Or south if you happened to be going south, of course.

In the bottom right corner of the screen a message box popped up.

"Whassup?"

"I'm good. Onto something here."

"Shoot."

"Not sure but I'm getting into a big system. Just don't know whose it is."

"Magic."

Tapping the keyboard, he scanned the lines of code, furrowing his brow. *Can't be....*

He went back to the messenger.

"You'll never believe this... I've hit the mother-fucking-lode!"

Death was feeling morose, which to those who knew him was pretty much his default emotion, so no change there, then. Since the IT crowd had taken over the darkness and his beloved hour glasses with their polished mahogany frames and engraved brass plates had been removed, all he had was a desk, laptop computer and a phone—although they allowed him to keep his horse, for which he was mildly grateful, if it was between gritted teeth. It was like being grateful to one's gaoler for letting you have bread and water twice a day, he grumbled to himself. Gone now the infinite corridors of lives all slipping though the neck of an elegant, timelessly designed hourglass, each unique and finite. Now lives were merely measured by the electrons in lines of computer code, faceless, soulless, bland and devoid of passion, devoid of style. The difference between Radio One and a Night at the Opera.

They didn't even allow the raven in to assist these days. Pets aren't allowed, he had been told, so the raven was now forced to remain outside. He could hear it cawing now, its plaintive cries coming through the window, tugging at his heartstrings. Well, they would have if he had any, but even so, somewhat unhappy with his lot, he found himself longing for the old days.

He sighed heavily and the tremor shivered through space and time, an echo of sadness for what once was, which was so much better than what was now. The raven cawed its agreement.

He took a sip of tea and grimaced. *Tea! Yuk!* There was a time when he would have been sipping a decent single malt, but they had banned him from drinking at work.

They will ban smoking next, he thought, just as a big friendly sign appeared all by itself on the wall opposite. In large red letters with a circle and a cigarette crossed through, it declared "Smoking is illegal on these premises." It also had a hand with the finger pointing directly at Death underneath which was written. "That means you."

Death swore to himself and wondered if those who called him the grim reaper might not have a point, for he was certainly feeling grim at this juncture. He picked up the smartphone that lay on his desk. He was sure that it was faulty. All day the screen had been freezing before doing a hard reset on its own. He wondered if he had missed any appointments. As he picked it up, it vibrated briefly before the screen went blank and the cycle started again.

"Bloody thing. Useless."

When it came back to life, he noticed that the battery was low.

"Hmm, less than 10%. Better put it on charge."

He fished around in the desk drawer and rooted out the charger. Having plugged it into the wall socket, he pushed the micro USB plug into the corresponding socket on the phone. The phone bleeped, the screen lit up and the room disappeared in a flash of light.

The hacker selected the messenger.

"I'm creating a new app with this stuff. We can wreak some havoc. Sending you the code."

"Awesome."

"Here is its."

"Fuck! Fucking fuckitty fuck! You know what this stuff is?"

"Yeah. Magic, innit?"

Death wondered where he was. It was dark. He still had his phone in his hand. No sign of the charger cable though. He shrugged and put it into the cavernous folds of his cape. Then a shimmer of light shot past him like an express locomotive and was gone. Then another came from an entirely different direction. He felt it as it passed. A waft of air and a slight tingling sensation then nothing.

"What…?"

"It's the machine," a voice said. Death looked around him just as another shimmering beam sped by, once more leaving a slight tingling in its wake.

"What?" He said again, unsure what else he could say.

"I said, it's the machine."

"What machine?"

"The machine. The machine that determines everything. Life, the universe and all time from the beginning to the end."

"Who are you?" It seemed to Death that his voice echoed slightly. He jumped as another arrow like light bolt zipped by, closely followed by another. *"What are these things?"*

"So many questions."

"Well, what do you expect?"

He thought he could feel the voice sighing with slight irritation as one would with a somewhat dense student who just does not get a simple mathematical sum, such as two plus two.

"I have no idea where I am nor how I got here."

"You are in the machine."

This time it was Death's turn to sigh.

"Four," he muttered to himself.

"I heard that."

Death was now growing irritable. *"Who are you?"*

"I am the mind of the machine."

"What machine?"

"The machine. This machine. The machine in which you are now in. Couldn't be plainer than the nose on my face."

Death felt that he was going round in circles. *"I can't see you let alone the nose on your face."*

"No need to get all pedantic."

As another beam of light shot towards him, Death lifted his scythe and struck at it, severing it in two. The two halves twisted and turned, bouncing in circles until they came to rest. He reached down and picked one up. At which point, an opening appeared above him, like a skylight in an attic.

"You shouldn't have done that."

"Oh, shut up!"

"You shouldn't speak to me like that!"

"Oh, boil your head!"

"I don't have a head."

"Well, boil something else then." Death found himself wondering where this entity kept its nose if it didn't have a head on which to keep it, but decided that the puzzle wasn't worth pursuing.

"No need to get all uppity."

Death grunted and looked up at the rectangular light. As he did so, he drifted up towards it as if mere thought could propel him, which apparently it did. Eventually, he could peer out…

"Oh, my…"

Gavin Reynolds leaned back from his computer screen and ran a hand through his grey hair. Page after page of spreadsheets were beginning to tire his eyes and his back ached. He stood and worked his shoulders around to loosen them up. *Time for a spot of refreshment,* he thought to himself and walked across to the drinks cabinet. Pulling out a bottle of brandy, he poured himself a generous glass and wandered back to the desk just as his phone buzzed and bleeped. Curious, he picked it up and frowned. "Hmmm, what is this?"

The text merely displayed a link. His curiosity getting the better of his common sense, he tapped a finger on it and watched as a download message appeared. Now he began to wonder if he had done the right thing, which he hadn't. Increasingly worried as the little bar moved along the screen, he tried to stop it in vain.

"Switch the damned thing off," he muttered to himself. He pressed the button on the side of the phone, but nothing happened. The bar moved inexorably across the screen, arriving eventually at the other side.

The screen went blank.

Then a message popped up.

"Happy Halloween, Your time has come."

"What?"

Death appeared on the screen, peering out at Gavin who clutched his chest, coughed and dropped dead. The phone still in his hand.

Death stepped back from the window as he watched Gavin fall to the ground and lay still. He felt a bit woozy as he spun around during the fall.

"How odd... How very odd indeed."

The window closed and once more he found himself in darkness.

Another shaft of light shot towards him and he struck it with the scythe.

"Oy!"

"Oh, get stuffed!"

"I don't like your attitude!"

"That's okay, I don't like yours." Death looked up and sure enough another window appeared in the darkness and he floated up to it and looked out.

The hacker watched the lines of code reading them as they shot across the screen. He clicked the messenger box.

"I can't believe this, it's working brilliantly."

"What are you doing now?"

"I have the power of life and death. Death is at my command. I've got another poor sap. About to snuff it. We can rule the world with this, assassinate anyone and Death can't stop us!"

"Awesome!"

Janice Weeks picked up her phone and watched the little bar as it moved across the screen.

Death watched as she died.

"This isn't right. It isn't right at all."

"Ask nicely."

"Ask what?"

"Ask me for help."

Death sighed.

"I heard that."

Death sighed more silently this time. It seemed to him that he was trapped here and needed the help of this entity whatever it was.

"Very well, I need your help."

As he stood there specks of light appeared from the darkness and coalesced, forming a human like shape that eventually resembled a young woman. She stood with her hands on her hips looking at him with a faint air of amusement mixed with disapproval. Death, meanwhile felt a mix of annoyance and relief that he could now see the owner of the disembodied voice and was at least pleasantly surprised to see that it wasn't too displeasing to look at—after all, he had seen some of the demons that lurked down below and they were no joke to look at. And, he thought to himself, their personal hygiene left something to be desired. Not that he had broached the subject with them.

"Ask me nicely. Say please," the entity commanded with just a hint of iron in her voice.

Death was growing irritated again.

"I can always go away again," the entity said.

"Okay, okay. Please will you help me? Whoever or whatever you are."

"I am the machine," she said. "I am random code. I exist everywhere and nowhere. I am life and time, the past, the present and the future. I can see all, hear all, and feel all. I am light and dark, joy and sadness, everything and nothing, omniscient and omnipresent. I am data. I am all."

"Modesty not being your strong point then?"

"I can always go away again and leave you here," she reminded him archly.

Death raised a hand apologetically, despite feeling anything but apologetic. It occurred to him that right at this moment a whisky and a cigarette would help his mood, but none were to be found.

"They are not allowed," the entity said as if reading his mind, which she was.

"Go on, explain what is happening here."

"You are inside your mobile phone. Your phone is connected through data streams to all other mobile phones…"

Death put two and two together and managed not to reach five. "The streams of light."

"Indeed, the streams of light. When you capture one, it takes you to someone's mobile phone. Hackers have broken into your system. Did you click on a link?"

"What's a link?"

"Oh, never mind. You are now trapped inside the data repository for every mobile phone in the universe. The windows you see are the screens of hacked phones. Then, when the owner looks at the screen, they see you along with a message."

"What message?"

"Happy Halloween, it's your time."

And it being their time, they die?"

"Well, you got there eventually."

"Thankyou. I think."

So it was beginning to make sense. But how to get out?

"Oh, that's easy."

"Well why didn't you tell me that when I arrived?"

"You didn't ask."

Death briefly considered giving her a swipe with his scythe but promptly strangled the thought before she could read it.

"I wouldn't if I were you."

Too late.

"Well?"

"Well, what?"

"Do you want to get out?"

"Of course I do!"

He refrained from voicing what else he wanted to say. The entity arched an eyebrow, which amused him as this was his trick.

"I know," she said. "I got it from you. Effective isn't it?"

"Can we...?"

"Follow me."

The entity rose gently into the air and Death felt himself being wafted up, although in the pitch black, up and down seemed to be much the same thing. As he drifted, he became aware that there were things floating around him. As he watched, they gelled into magenta skulls with bright red glowing eyes wafting and drifting in the darkness. Some of them burst and vanished then another would appear from nowhere.

"What?"

"Oh, ignore them, they are just possibilities that may happen or not. I take no notice of them and they usually go away."

Eventually they could see a light far away. As it grew closer, Death could see that it was another window.

"Someone's computer screen?" He asked.

"Yes. Keep following me."

The hacker watched as the little virus he had set loose worked its way through the system, infecting one phone after another. So far only two deaths and he was wondering what the delay was. He reached for the messenger box to contact his collaborator when his phone buzzed. Absently, he reached for it and picked it up and looked at the screen.

"Hello," said Death. *"You weren't expecting me, were you? Happy Halloween."* He swung his scythe. There was a flash of light and Death found himself standing next to the inert corpse of the

hacker slumped over his computer keyboard, the beer from the tipped over can running across it, causing the screen to stutter and go blank. In his hand was a mobile phone.

"Well, that seems to have worked."

"Think nothing of it," said a voice in his head. "Anytime."

"Thank you."

"There, that wasn't too hard, was it?"

Death grunted.

He thought he could hear a chuckle. "Happy Halloween to you, too."

Death laughed to himself. He decided that annoying though it was, the entity amused him and he liked her. A little bit of him was sorry to see her go.

He reached in his cloak for his phone. He raised one of his non-existent eyebrows. The machine must have charged it, he thought to himself.

"Think nothing of it."

"Well, thanks anyway." An appointment popped up on the screen. He sighed.

"No peace for the wicked, eh?"

The Wisdom of Cnut

Mark Ellott

AD 1020 or thereabouts…
Somewhere by the sea.

The courtiers gathered on the beach. Two of them carrying the heavy, ornate chair, stumbling slightly under its weight as they walked. The king followed as they made their way across the sand walking awkwardly as it shifted beneath their feet, lifting the hems of their robes to keep them from the sand until they reached the more firm shoreline wetted by the incoming tides with hard little ripples left by the receding waves.

"Here," Cnut ordered. "This will do, place it right here."

The courtiers did as he commanded and set the throne down and stood aside as Cnut took a seat and waited. The tide was on its way in.

Above them in the dunes, unobserved by the small party on the shore, a small fair haired child of about ten peered through the marram grass watching as she observed a moment in history.

Death sat down next to her as the raven circled overhead cawing to anyone who would listen, which was no one.

"Interesting stuff, eh?"

She looked at him. "Are you the grim reaper?

"Why does everyone call me grim?"

"Well," she said, "I expect that it is because being dead is no joke."

"Such wisdom from one so young. I might use that. I like it."

"I am Alfhild," she announced. "What should I call you?"

"Very pleased to meet you, Alfhild. You may call me Death."

"Am I about to die?"

"Oh, no, you have a long time yet, Alfhild. But, like all innocents, you can see me." He changed the subject. *"So what is going on down on the beach?"*

"The king is to command the sea not to come in."

"What do you think will happen?"

"I think that he will get his feet wet, silly man."

Death chuckled. *"Alfhild, Cnut is as wise as you are. He knows he will get his feet wet."*

"Then why is he doing it?"

"Because," Death said, *"He is proving a point."*

Alfhild frowned as she thought about this. "What point is that? I can't see any point in getting your feet wet."

"Cnut knows what his courtiers seem not to; that there are some things in Heaven and Earth that man cannot control and that God does not give kings any special powers."

"But surely God decreed that he should be the king."

"God, my dear, has other things to deal with than who is the king on some small, damp outpost on the edge of an insignificant continent on a little blue planet on the outskirts of the Milky Way. He barely knows the place exists. If he did, he would probably need a map to find it."

"I have no idea what you are on about."

Death sighed. *"No, my dear, you don't. But it is of no concern now. Just watch the entertainment."*

At that moment, Cnut leapt out of his chair and stepped back from the water now encroaching on his feet. They watched as he remonstrated with his courtiers.

"Let all men know how empty and worthless is the power of kings, for there is none worthy of the name, but He whom heaven, earth, and sea obey by eternal laws."

"He means God," Death said, standing now, using his scythe as a support. He groaned at the effort. *"Old bones,"* he explained. *"Mark well what you have seen today, for this is a momentous day in history."*

"Really? The king getting wet feet?" Alfhild watched him as he stood and the raven fluttered about overhead, cawing impatiently.

"An appointment," he said. *"No peace for the wicked, eh?"*

"Will I see you again?

"Count on it, my dear, you may count on it."

London, 1665.

October was about pass into November and the sky was bleak. A low evening mist rolled in, shrouding the last of the mourners in the graveyard. Death stepped down from his horse and looked about. There was a mournful silence that blanketed the landscape, broken only by the groans of the bereaved, mourning for the losses of so many loved ones. The stench of plague hung heavy on the air. A little girl sat on a bench by the entrance to the cemetery. She watched as a cloaked man walked by, his face hidden by his bird-like mask. She turned as Death walked up and sat next to her. The raven cawed irritably at the man in the mask.

"Now, now," Death chided it. *"He isn't after your job."*

The raven fluttered its wings and folded them down on its back, its beady eyes fixed upon the human imposter as he walked among the mist shrouded graves, tapping the ground with his staff.

Despite Death's admonishment, he wasn't about to let this one out of his sight, just in case.

"What a funny man," the girl said.

"Him or me?" Death asked.

She turned to look at him and wrinkled her nose. "Well, now that you mention it…"

"I suppose that I asked for that," Death said as he settled alongside her. Despite being poorly dressed, she was in fine health with rosy cheeks and bright eyes below a mop of unruly dark hair. "My name's Molly," she said by way of introduction.

"I know."

"Have we met before? I feel that we have."

Death waved a hand briefly in front of her face and the memories came flooding back. Of a beach and the tide coming in and a king getting his feet wet.

"Oh, yes, I remember. It was a long time ago."

"You are an old soul, my dear. You have been here before. Many times, in fact."

As they watched the mourners gather together and walk towards the entrance of the desolate graveyard, they could see a lone rider making his way towards them. Pestilence drew to a stop and lifted a hand in greeting. "I have been busy creating work for you," he said to Death, a toothless grin failing to light up his ashen face, his horse pawing the ground impatiently.

"I thought you were going to get those teeth seen to," Death said, ignoring the reason for Pestilence's visit.

"Ha! That circle of Hell is one place I am reluctant to visit. Still, I must be off. Plenty to do, doncha know?" With that, he nudged his horse and rode off, the mist enveloping him until he had vanished completely, leaving a faint odour of decay in his wake.

"I don't like him very much," Molly said.

"Who does?" Death replied. *"I, on the other had... Yes often I am welcomed."*

"Why is everyone dying?"

"It's the plague."

"Well, I know that, silly! What I mean is why are we dying? Why can't the king stop it instead of running away?"

Death sighed. *From the mouths of babes*, he thought to himself. *"Kings have the luxury of running away. The rest of you must remain and take your chances, but the king cannot stop this any more than Cnut could stop the waves from getting his feet wet. There will come a time when men can cure diseases like this, but that time has not come."*

"So the king was right to run away."

Death shrugged. *"Maybe. But this disease is not carried upon the air, so unless he allows rats into his palaces, he would be fine. This ailment is borne in blood carried by the fleas that infest the rats."*

"But what of us? The poor? The rats are all around us."

The raven cawed. The plague doctor was coming back from the far side of the cemetery. The raven fixed him with a glare, but the masked man took no notice, being unable to see the bird or Death. He walked by absorbed in his thoughts until he, too was gone in the mist, the tap, tap tapping of his cane echoing in the fading light.

"Ah," Death said sadly. *"The poor will always take the brunt of these things. It is the way. It always has been, but mark my words, the king will not escape me."* He tapped the scythe with meaning. *"Everyone gets their appointment with me, no matter how gilded their palaces may be, no matter how wealthy or powerful. All must face the reaper and all are equal to me."*

Molly thought about his answer for a moment. "Surely the king could do something?"

Death fished a clay pipe out of his cloak and set about the task of filing the bowl with tobacco and fiddling with a tinder box to light it. Eventually he got it going and breathed in the sweet smelling smoke.

"If he knew what to do, then yes, he could do something. Cleaning up the squalor would help. Getting rid of most of London would help, but..." He lapsed into silence.

"What?"

"Oh, you will find out soon enough. But worry not, you will be around for a few decades yet."

"Then I will see you again one day?"

"Oh, yes. One day."

He stood and leaned against his scythe. He paused and looked down at her. *"Live well, my dear. Until I see you again."*

October, 2020.

The twenty-first century wasn't all it was cracked up to be, Death decided. Not only all this new technology, that he found more irritating than useful, but it occurred to him sometimes that things were going backwards.

October was just about to hand over the reins to November and the sky was dull, heavy with the portent of rain or maybe worse. Certainly there was that bone aching chill to the atmosphere, so it would be no surprise.

He rode steadily looking for someone. Eventually, he found her sitting on a bench in the park. Someone had put tape across it with a notice announcing that it was no longer in use so as to allow for social distancing. But the tape had been torn asunder and the notice flapped impotently in the light breeze ignored by the occupant. As he sat next to her and leaned his scythe against the bench, he wondered if the child was the rebel in question. Although she was wearing a face mask, so not too rebellious he assumed.

"Did you do this?" he asked.

"Yes," she said. "It was a silly thing. This is a park, with a pond and ducks and things. How is sitting or not sitting making any difference to social distancing?"

He looked at her. She was blonde again this time. *"What is your name now?"* he asked.

"Susan," she said. "We've met before, haven't we? You said that I am an old soul."

"Yes, I did. And now you are here."

He paused as Pestilence rode up and stopped alongside them. He still hadn't done anything about his teeth, Death noted absently, nor the body odour.

"I've been busy again," he announced. "Got to give you something to do." He looked about him expansively, pleased with his work.

Death looked up and despised the smugness in his tone. *"Less than a million worldwide?"* he snorted. *"It's not exactly 1665, is it?"*

Pestilence pulled on the reins and harrumphed. "No pleasing some!"

He turned the horse and rode off.

"I don't like him at all," Susan said.

"Yes, you said."

For a moment or two they watched the ducks. The raven squawked, but they ignored him.

"Why are you wearing a mask?" Death asked eventually.

"To stop the spread of the disease," she replied.

"So how does that work?" he asked.

"If I sneeze, it stops the virus from getting out."

"Have you sneezed?"

"Well, no, but if I did…"

"If you did, what would happen?"

She laughed. "I'd probably get a face full of snot!"

"That sounds nice," Death said pulling a face even though he had no muscles to pull it. *"Then what?"*

Susan frowned as she thought through the mechanics of sneezing in a mask. "I suppose," she said, "I'd be sneezing into my ears. It would come out of the sides."

Death fiddled around in the folds of his cloak and extracted a cigarette. He went through the motions of tapping it and putting it into his mouth before flicking a Zippo and pulling the flame into the tobacco. He breathed in and exhaled a stream of smoke. *"So what good will sneezing into your ears do? Will that stop the disease?"*

"It's what the government has told us to do," she said as if that was a trump card.

"Ah. Yes. The government. Wise men are they?"

"I suppose so," she said slowly. She pulled a face. "My mother called them all sorts of rude words and she doesn't think they are very clever at all, which is a bit confusing, because if they aren't very clever, why are they in charge?"

Death laughed. He smoked in silence for a few moments before stubbing the cigarette out and crushing it under his foot.

"You can't leave that there, the litter police will give you a fine."

"It's a virtual cigarette. I am an ethereal being made of ectoplasm and no one but you and cats can see me."

The raven squawked. *"And you. I haven't forgotten you."*

Death followed its gaze to where a small black cat had paused in licking its nether regions to stare at him. He smiled and waved a hand whereupon the cat twitched its whiskers and resumed snuffling about somewhere disgusting.

Susan decided that maybe this one was best left where it was and lapsed into silence as she turned her attention back to the ducks.

"I remember 1969. There was a pandemic then, too."

"What happened?"

"Lots of people went to Woodstock during that summer as it was at its peak. It was a music festival. They still talk about it today."

"I know. Granny talks about it."

"Well, there you are then."

"Did they wear masks to stop the disease?"

"No." Death fished around in his cloak again and pulled out a small flask. He unscrewed the top and took a swig, savouring the warm glow from the amber coloured liquid. *"Ahhh. The good stuff. They put a man on the moon in 1969, too."* It was taking time, but he was eventually getting to his point.

"What has that got to do with the disease?" Susan was baffled by Death's apparent mental meandering and was wondering if he was going senile.

"There was a joke doing the rounds."

"Well, what was it?"

"We have put a man on the moon, they said, but we can't cure the common cold."

Susan looked at him poker-faced. "That's not very funny."

"Not all jokes are."

"Jokes are supposed to be funny. If it doesn't make you laugh, how can it be a joke?"

"Not," Death said, *"If they are making a satirical point. Then they don't have to be funny at all, they just need to make you think."*

"What am I supposed to think about curing the common cold?"

"It's a corona virus. So is the flu."

"And so is Covid."

"Indeed," Death said, satisfied that Susan was getting it.

"But we cured other diseases, so why the big thing about the common cold?"

Death was warming to his subject now. *"Remember the plague back in 1665? Well, that was a bacterium. Man learned how to cure that with antibiotics that kill the bacteria that cause the disease. He also learned that hygiene is useful for disease prevention. Man has also invented cures and vaccines to kill viruses. But some viruses are too difficult to cure."*

"Why?"

"It's in their DNA. Corona viruses have only one strand, not two. You know what DNA is?"

Susan pulled a face. "Of course. It has a helix."

"But not corona viruses," he said. *"That's what makes them such annoying little buggers. Without that second strand, there is nothing stopping them mutating. Everyone is hoping for a vaccine, which will arrive, of course, but like the flu vaccine, it will only be partially effective. It all depends on the strain."*

"So what should we do? All the governments in the world are telling us to stay home or wear masks when we are out to stay safe. They are in charge and know what to do."

Ah, the innocence of a child, Death thought to himself. *"Governments are run by politicians,"* he said. *"Politicians are generally fools and buffoons who think they know more than they do. Worse than kings, I sometimes think. They rely on experts who have their own agendas—usually to do with funding. He who pays the piper and all that. So they tell the politicians what they think the politicians want to hear, but the politicians don't always know what they want to hear and have little idea what to do with it if they did."*

He took another swig of the whisky and lapsed into silence as he pondered the state of the world. Man was supposed to be the apex predator, top of the food chain, highly evolved, yet sometimes hive animals such as bees and ants made more sense to him. Why even his raven had a wisdom far beyond the reach of the average politician, who knew only the continuous yearning for power, control and position. Although why they would want it as it was a constant struggle to keep it and you grow old before your years with the strain, he wondered. Yes, he concluded, worse, even than kings. Mankind was an enigma.

"So what should we do?" Susan was saying.

"Nothing."

"Nothing? But lots of people will die."

"People will die anyway. It is the nature of the world."

"That is a cruel thing to say."

"Is it? I thought it was pragmatic. Look, here is the thing, politicians cannot control an airborne pathogen. A century and a half ago, they learned how to stop cholera by ensuring clean drinking water. That is controllable. But the very air itself? That's another matter. Although..." He lapsed as his train of thought took a tangent. *"Man can control the pollutants he puts into the air. But the air itself and a microscopic thing that is floating about that he cannot see? No, he cannot control that any more than Cnut could control the tide. So, yes, do nothing very much. Let me get on with my job..."*

"I think I might have gone off you," Susan scolded. "You are heartless and cruel."

"Life is heartless and cruel, but it can also be joyous and magical," he replied. *"You have to make the best of what you have and be happy with it. Everyone has their appointment with me eventually."*

Death stood and picked up his scythe. Lifting himself into the saddle, he looked down at her. *"One day, my dear, you will understand what you once knew to be true a thousand years ago. That some things are beyond the ability of human beings to control. That some things are best adapted to rather than controlled. God no more gives politicians super powers than he did kings. They are all flesh and blood and flawed to boot. Understand that and life is simpler that way."*

"And for some, shorter," she said.

Death inclined his head conceding the point. *"Yes, for some. But then, it always was."*

He pulled on the reins and turned away, riding out of her life until her final appointment and she watched him go.

The evening light cast long shadows on the beach. The sea was calm, the waves gently lapping the shore. As the sun dipped below the horizon, the stratosphere turned purple. Alone on the sand facing out to sea was an ornate chair. A throne. And on the throne sat a solitary figure, staring out to sea, watching the tide come in.

Death rode steadily, his horse's hooves leaving prints in the damp sand. Eventually he arrived at the throne and dismounted.

Cnut looked at him as he stood by the throne and looked out to the horizon, taking in the blissful view and gentle lapping of the waves.

"Well," Cnut said. "It's been a while."

"A thousand years, give or take."

"That long, eh? Much must have happened in that time."

Oh, it has. Man can now fly to the heavens. They put a man on the moon, you know."

"A man on the moon! Such wonder!"

"Aye, many wonders have I seen in my time. Mankind never ceases to amaze me with his adaptability and his inventiveness. There are so many things that have happened since your time, it would take me another thousand years to tell you of them."

"A thousand years!" Cnut said, allowing his imagination to try and see what Death had seen. He sat back in the throne, his eyes fixed upon something in his mind, of the world a thousand years hence and what wonders it might hold that were beyond his meagre imaginings. "And by that time, men must have learned great wisdom."

Death placed a hand on his shoulder and sighed.

"Ah, well, steady on old chap, let's not be too hasty…"

Afterword

Roo B. Doo

I left writing this Afterword for as long as I can, Dear Reader. I don't know what to say about 2020 – *so far* - other than that Western Civilisation seems to have slipped from 'Flatten the Curve' into Covid-1984 Marshall Law, with horrifying speed. If that doesn't scare you, we sincerely hope the tales contained within volume 12 have done the trick ;)

The poem offered on the Afterword mutilating slab this time round comes from the pen of black American poet, novelist and playwright, Paul Laurence Dunbar (1872 - 1906). His parents were slaves before the Civil War and he died from TB aged 33. He went to school with Wilbur and Orville Wright, and his poem 'We Wear The Mask' needed only the barest tweaking to bring it up slap up to date.

See you for Christmas, Dear Reader, unless it's cancelled.

We Wear The Mask

We wear the mask to save our lives,
It hides our fears and shades their lies—
This price we pay for elected guile;
With torn and bleeding hearts they smile,
Mouth rules with myriad subtleties.

Why should the NHS be over-wise,
Count our temperature lows and highs?
Nay, let them only see us, while
We wear the mask.

We clap, but, O great Covid, their cries
From thee all recorded deaths arise.
We sigh, but oh this way is vile
Beneath our feet, the hellish mile;
We trudge and dream otherwise,
We wear the mask!

About the Authors

Gayle Fidler

Gayle Fidler is a writer, collector of bad taxidermy, paranormal researcher, part time pirate and make-up artist. She is also a Viking blacksmith who likes to hand forge spoons and toasting forks.

Gayle lives in the North East of England with several cats and several children. She is married to her best friend Ben, who lives 100 miles away from her in Yorkshire because he likes to sleep with all the windows open.

Gayle began writing on the back of beer mats to try and make up reasonable excuses for some of the ridiculous situations her and Ben found themselves in during drunken capers.

Wandra Nomad

Born well infused – perhaps some would say overly infused – with wanderlust and curiosity, Wandra Nomad has traversed much of the globe, exploring a myriad of customs and cultures while participating in diverse opportunistic pursuits including a multitude of occupations that helped fund said treks.

Also born an unbridled dreamer, this wanderer has traveled even further in imagination. The results of this combination are innumerable diverse 'tales to be told', one of which is offered in this Anthology. There are more in Wandra's own collection, 'Musings of a Wanderer', available now.

Having sampled a variety of climates ranging from freezing ice and snow to steaming jungles along the way a definite preference has developed. Today many such tales are spun by the Muse on the beaches around the tropical belt before wending their way to this nomad's keyboard.

Marsha Webb

Marsha lives just outside Cardiff and is a full time high school teacher. She has only recently started writing.

"Writing short stories are my favourite because teaching takes up so much time and because I love the feeling of achievement when a story is finished. I have always had a very over active imagination and writing allows me to use this in a positive way."

Marsha also has stories in Underdog Anthologies 6, 7, 8, 9 and 10 and has had a number of short stories and poems published in online magazines and themed anthologies.

Her first novel 'You Can Choose Your Sin… but you cannot choose the consequences' is now available in print and eBook formats.

Daniel Royer

Daniel Royer is a writer of short fiction. He is a California State University, Bakersfield graduate with an English Degree he's not using. Royer works as a full-time welder to support his true passion, which is tomahawk-throwing. His stories have been printed by Ponahakeola Press, SFReader.com, The Sirens Call, and some other publications you've never heard of. He used to have a cat.

Mark Ellott

Mark Ellott is a part time motorcycle instructor, delivering training for students who require compulsory basic training and direct access courses. He has retired from his main job as a freelance trainer and assessor working primarily in the rail industry, delivering track safety training and assessment as well as providing consultancy services in competence management.

He writes fiction in his spare time. Mostly, his fiction consists of short stories crossing a range of genres, and has stories in all but one of the previous Underdog Anthologies – and now in this one.

His first three novels, 'Ransom', 'Rebellion' and 'Resolution', are now available in print and eBook formats.

He has also published a volume of his own short stories, entitled 'Blackjack', and a collection of Morning Cloud Western stories entitled 'Sinistré'. Another short story collection is currently in preparation for publication.

Roo B. Doo

Just the one offering from me this Halloween, Dear Reader. Enjoy!

Want more Roob? You can find her on the internet, ably assisted by Clicky, who may or may not be a) an alien dolphin and b) from another dimension, lolling about her Library of Libraries, writing synchromystic shambles at www.roobeedoo2.wordpress.com

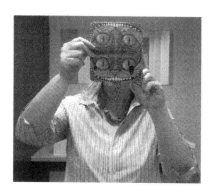

Emma Townsend

Emma has previously worked as a medical secretary, bingo caller and silk screen printer. Currently, she is a 'homemaker', despite having made no homes whatsoever, can't cook and deeply resents the laundry.

She lives in Lincolnshire with her partner and their young daughter.

H. K. Hillman

H. K. Hillman is the creator, or perhaps creation, of Romulus Crowe, Dr. Phineas Dume and Legiron the Underdog. Now pretty much retired from science, he hides out in an ancient farmhouse in Scotland with a Viking who calls herself CynaraeStMary. The house includes a skull in a holly tree, a gallows stone in the wall and holy water comes out of all the taps.

Here he spends a lot of time thinking up horrible stories, and running the tiny publishing house called Leg Iron Books, helped by Roo B. Doo, who he's never met.

No, he doesn't understand how any of this happened either.

LEG IRON BOOKS

Also available from Leg Iron Books:

Underdog Anthologies

'The Underdog Anthology, volume 1'
'Tales the Hollow Bunnies Tell' (anthology II)
'Treeskull Stories' (anthology III)
'The Good, the Bad and Santa' (anthology IV)
'Six in Five in Four' (anthology V)
'The Gallows stone' (anthology VI)
'Christmas Lights… and Darks' (anthology VII)
'Transgenre Dreams' (anthology VIII)
'Well Haunted' (anthology IX)
'The Silence of the Elves' (anthology X)
'Tales from Loch Doon' (anthology XI)
              All edited by H.K. Hillman and Roo B. Doo.

Fiction

'The Goddess of Protruding Ears' by Justin Sanebridge
'De Godin van de Flaporen' by Justin Sanebridge (in Dutch)
'Ransom', by Mark Ellott
'Rebellion' by Mark Ellott
'Resolution' by Mark Ellott
'Blackjack' a collection of short stories by Mark Ellott
'Sinistré (The Morning Cloud Chronicles)' by Mark Ellott
'The Mark' by Margo Jackson
'You'll be Fine' by Lee Bidgood
'Feesten onder de Drinkboom' by Dirk Vleugels (in Dutch)
'Es-Tu là, Allah?' by Dirk Vleugels (in French)
'Jessica's Trap' by H.K. Hillman
'Samuel's Girl' by H.K. Hillman
'Norman's House' by H. K. Hillman
'The Articles of Dume' by H.K. Hillman

'Fears of the Old and the New' short stories by H.K. Hillman
'Dark Thoughts and Demons' short stories by H.K. Hillman
'You Can Choose Your Sin… but You Cannot Choose the Consequences' by Marsha Webb
'Musings of a Wanderer' short stories by Wandra Nomad

Non-fiction:

'Ghosthunting for the Sensible Investigator' first and second editions, by Romulus Crowe

Biography:

'Han Snel' by Dirk Vleugels (in Dutch)

Printed in Great Britain
by Amazon

27334840R00084